Dead List

# Helen H. Durrant

# DEAD LIST

*Detectives Calladine & Bayliss Book 3*

JOFFE BOOKS

Revised edition 2025
Joffe Books, London
www.joffebooks.com

Previously published as *A Deadly Imperfection*
by H.H. Durrant in 2015

First published as *Dead List* by Joffe Books in 2015

Cover art by Nick Castle

ISBN: 978-1-80573-029-3

# PROLOGUE

The elderly woman thrust a sheet of paper at Tariq Ahmed through the open door. She wasn't smiling.

"I'm sorry to disturb you," she said, and her voice quivered with emotion. "I've lost my cat. I'm going to all the houses in the road." She showed him the printed photo. "He's been gone almost a week and I think someone must have taken him in."

She was small, slightly red-faced with a long thin nose on which perched a pair of old fashioned spectacles. Doctor Tariq Ahmed, who wasn't smiling either, shook his head in annoyance. It had been a long hard day. All he wanted was some well-earned peace and quiet. "Sorry — I can't help." He gave the image a cursory glance and dismissed her with a wave of his hand. "And don't drop that on my drive on your way out," he told her, attempting to shut the door.

But the old woman let out a loud sob and grabbed hold of his arm as she teetered on her feet. "Please. I have to find him — he's all I've got and he'll pine."

"Use your stick. Lean on that, it's what it's for," he told her sharply, trying to prise her fingers off his arm. "You should go home. It's dark and cold. Even your cat will have better sense than to wander the streets on a night like this."

1

Something about the way she looked wasn't quite right. Her hair was odd and her clothes were too big, but he was too irritated to work out why that might be.

He made to close the door again but this time she flopped forward. "I feel woozy," she gasped, breathlessly. "I know I shouldn't be out; I've got a bad chest. But I have to find him. Could I have a glass of water, please, take one of my tablets? Then I'll go."

Tariq Ahmed narrowed his eyes, staring at the woman. She looked old and frail; he was a doctor after all, so despite his annoyance at being disturbed he felt compelled to help. With an impatient sigh, he turned and went back down his hallway to the kitchen, leaving her at the door.

* * *

Harriet Finch smiled. This was easier than she'd imagined. In a few paces she was inside. Taking care to follow him quietly, she was at his back in seconds.

She pressed a catch on her walking stick, releasing a wicked-looking blade like a bayonet. It was a nifty little gadget inherited from her grandfather and had languished unused for years in her hall cupboard. When she remembered it was there she'd given it an overhaul. Now it was a fine weapon.

She raised the stick high. If the doctor had looked up, he would have seen her shadow etched on the wall. But he didn't, and before he realised what was happening she had plunged the blade into the centre of his back.

It slid in, almost like a knife into butter at first, but then it stuck. There was something hard in the way — vertebrae? Harriet let out a loud grunt of annoyance, her arm twisting and pushing against the obstruction. Finally she was rewarded with a satisfying little crunch as the blade slid the last few inches deep into his body.

He didn't even turn. She watched his arms flail wildly and heard him utter a feeble little groan. She almost laughed

2

when he clutched his side and with one last wail pitched forward, headlong onto the floor.

Harriet's aim was true — he was done for. Another flick of her thumb and the blade retracted. Perfect. All she had to do now was the last bit, so the police would get things right. Over the coming days Harriet was going to carry out a number of murders and they would all be different. She didn't want to be a nuisance. Of course they'd investigate, they'd have to. But she didn't want them chasing their tails looking for multiple killers.

She took a single, six-inch nail and a hammer from her bag and fished in her pocket for the card. Taking care not to get blood on her clothes, she pushed Doctor Ahmed onto his back. She placed the card against his closed right eye and positioned the nail. With one powerful stroke of the hammer she forced the metal deep into his skull through the eye socket, fixing the card in place. A tarot card on each of the bodies would be her signature. The police would link the killings, which would make it easier for them in the end.

Harriet didn't want to tarry but she couldn't help being curious. After all, this was the man who'd started it; he was so cold and had no empathy whatsoever. Over the last few months she'd come to hate him. Since she was here she wanted to see how he lived, what made him tick.

She wandered idly from room to room, eyeing the casual elegance of the furnishings. He had good taste and obviously enjoyed having nice things around him. Of course with his job he could afford them. His walls were covered in paintings, some she recognised as the work of local artists.

His sitting room was dimly lit; there was only one small lamp on a table, but something glinted, catching her eye. It was a gold envelope addressed to Doctor T. Ahmed. Harriet picked it up and looked inside. The envelope contained two invitations to an art exhibition to be held later that week at the Leesworth Community Centre. She hadn't bought her friend Nesta's birthday present yet, and Nesta was an art lover. The invite said there'd be food and wine. Nesta would like that too. Harriet put the envelope in her pocket and went back into the kitchen.

There was a large pool of blood forming around the body. She smiled to herself. This was good, very good, and so much better than sitting around at home moping. And it was only fitting that he should be the first. After all, it was he who had given her the grim news. So it served him right, the heartless bastard.

She leaned forward to check that the image on the tarot card could be clearly seen. 'The Tower,' otherwise known as 'the bolt from the blue.' How very apt. Doctor Tariq Ahmed certainly hadn't seen it coming.

# CHAPTER 1

*Tuesday*

"So you can't even give us a date?" Ruth asked, as she helped herself to another grape from the bag on the sofa, where Tom Calladine lay sprawled. "Or perhaps you don't want to," she suggested with a frown on her face. "If I didn't know you better, I'd say you were swinging the lead. So come on then, come clean — what has the doctor said? Your injuries weren't really that bad, were they? It's just that work is piling up and we were short-handed before you went and got . . . well, before you got yourself shot," she said soberly.

"You're a hard woman, Ruth Bayliss. You'd have me out of my sick bed and back at my desk without a second thought, ready or not."

"Ready!" she scoffed. "OK, your arm caught a bullet, but come on, Tom, it barely winged you."

"Thanks to Lydia's quick thinking," he told her pointedly. "Without that woman's timely intervention things might be very different now." He sniffed.

Ruth rolled her eyes — he was really milking it.

"You got shot and you knocked yourself out when you hit the floor. Surely even you must have recovered by now.

5

Think about the timescale — all that was over two months ago. So . . . I have to ask, what's stopping you?"

"I broke my arm too, don't forget that." He snatched up his grapes and stuffed the bag behind a cushion, out of her reach.

"If I didn't know you better, Tom Calladine, I'd say you'd become a tad work-shy," she suggested and took a step back out of his reach.

"Like I said — a hard woman," he grimaced, picking up the cushion and throwing it at her. "You've got some cheek. I'd like to see you apprehend a villain with an arm like mine."

"If that's all that's bothering you, then I'll do the apprehending, and you can come back and do the thinking. Seriously though, we really do need you. It's crap at the nick right now. Jones got the push — don't even bother asking me what happened because no one's talking. So what do they do? They put Brad Long in charge! Brad *bloody* Long, for heaven's sake. Called him 'acting DCI' and stuck him in Jones's office."

"That bad, eh? Well, looks like you could certainly do with a bailout."

"Too bloody true we could. So when can we expect you?"

She was willing him to say the right thing. Life at the coalface was no fun at the moment, and without Tom it would only get worse.

But Tom Calladine didn't get time to answer. Ruth went to see who it was knocking on his front door.

\*\*\*

"Rocco!" he called out to the young detective constable. "Great to see you. Get yourself a coffee or something and join us." He nodded in the direction of the kitchen.

"Sorry, sir, it's Ruth that I need to see," DC Simon Rockliffe's face was serious — this was obviously no social call.

"We've got a major incident on our hands — at Hopecross," he explained. "A consultant from City Hospital

6

in Manchester was found dead on his kitchen floor this morning."

"You should have rung," Ruth told him.

"Well, I'm glad you didn't," Calladine piped up. "Not only is it good to see you but now you can give us both the grisly details. I presume it is murder?"

"Yep — stabbed in the back and there's something else — something rather creepy. The poor guy had a playing card nailed to his head — can you believe that? Goodness knows what it means, but it's already looking like a real head-scratcher."

"Anything else?" Calladine was sitting up now.

"Not that I know of but we need to get down there quick," he said, turning to face Ruth. "Long's sent DS Thorpe to the scene but he'll miss more than he notices."

"I'm getting pretty sick of having to cover his back. The man's a menace and a real lazy sod. He's sticking his nose in everywhere and all because it was his DI that got the leg up." Ruth folded her arms, looking long and hard at Calladine. "It should have been you, you know. Fallon or no Fallon, you're the best man for the job. The whole nick knows it."

But Calladine knew Ruth was wrong. It was all about Ray Fallon. Fallon was a criminal, awaiting trial for murder and, as far as everyone knew, the man was his cousin! If he wanted to move ahead in his career, he'd have to come clean and do something about the information he was sitting on.

"What about this new case, then? How are you going to tackle it?" He pointedly did not reply to Ruth's observation about Fallon.

"Well, if you got your arse off that sofa, you could come with us. Once Thorpe sees you've reappeared he'll back off, so will Long," Ruth suggested, tapping her foot.

"That's no way to speak to your DI, Sergeant," Calladine retorted.

"Well, you're not, are you? Not at the moment anyway."

"Hopecross, you said?" Calladine reached for a notepad on his coffee table and hastily scribbled a couple of lines. "Just letting Lydia know where I've gone. She worries," he confided with a grin.

"Quite the little housewife," Ruth noted sarcastically. "Got you wrapped round her little finger good and proper. I bet it's down to her that you've stayed home with your feet up all this time."

"What if it is? I like being wrapped round her little finger," he smirked. "I like her being here — she's been brilliant."

And she had. Despite reservations about her housekeeping skills, she'd come up with the goods where it counted. She'd been his nurse, his cook; she'd sorted out his finances and even advised his daughter about her problems when he'd been still groggy from the morphine.

"She got you into this mess. Or have you forgotten it was she who went tearing after your renegade cousin and brought him back here, gun in hand?"

"Fallon was after me before Lydia stuck her nose in. He knew it was me that got the evidence to finally convict him. I was always going to be his target."

"Any excuse for not seeing things as they are," she sighed. "Do you want to help with this, or what?"

"I could take a look. I suppose it can't do any harm."

"My car, then — I promise to bring you home afterwards."

"I'll get my coat."

* * *

The massive detached stone house was set in a leafy lane bordering the village of Hopecross — very different from his own tiny cottage in the back streets of Leesdon. Calladine wondered how much it would cost to run a place like this — too much most likely. But then their victim was a big-shot doctor, so he could probably afford it.

Amidst the heavy uniformed presence, Calladine spotted the pathologist, Doctor Sebastian Hoyle and the senior forensic scientist, Doctor Julian Batho. He hadn't seen them in quite a while.

"Good to have you back, Tom!" Doc Hoyle shouted to him, a big smile on his face. "If you are back that is. You had us worried for a while," he said, handing out white, paper suits. "You never know with knocks to the head. Are you on this one? Only DS Thorpe was here earlier but I don't think he stayed above two minutes."

"Yes, Doc, this one's mine," Calladine confirmed. "And yes, I think I might be back, finally. I've certainly missed it," he said, matching the pathologist's grin.

Doc Hoyle nodded. "He's been dead since last night, no later. His cleaning lady found him earlier this morning. Poor woman, she's been carted off to the General in shock."

Calladine pulled on the suit, donned a pair of overshoes and a mask and followed Doc Hoyle into the house.

"According to Ruth I've not showed my face a minute too soon," he told the doc. "She's getting a bit lippy about the situation at work, and to be honest, I've had enough of being an invalid."

"As long as you're up to it. This job's no picnic even when things are slack."

"Picnic or not, I need to get back. My brain's going to porridge. I'm in serious danger of losing my edge."

Tariq Ahmed was lying on the floor. The pool of blood had seeped from the small kitchen out into the hallway.

"One stab wound to the back. The post-mortem should throw some light on what was used but it was a long blade, I'd say. The volume of blood loss suggests one of the major arteries has been severed — possibly the aorta."

"There are plenty of prints. We'll start checking them out as soon as, but I'll lay odds they belong to him." Julian nodded at the body. "My bet is that our man wore gloves," he added. "We'll bag everything and take what we find back to the lab."

"Did you give DS Thorpe the details?"

"He didn't stay long enough." Julian smirked. "He had a quick look round and decided he'd be better off going back to the nick."

So Ruth had been right.

"Any sign of the murder weapon?"

"Don't think we're going to be that lucky, Inspector," Julian told him.

"What do we know about Doctor Ahmed?" Calladine asked Rocco.

"Nothing yet, sir, other than he worked at the City. I'm going to start having a proper look round, see if he had any close family but I get the impression from uniform, who've been talking to the neighbours, that he lived alone."

"What about the neighbours? Someone should find out if they saw or heard anything."

"One of the uniformed PCs has already been down the road asking," Ruth said, as she joined them inside. "Apparently they heard nothing. Mind you these properties are big and spaced well apart. Anything could go on and I doubt the neighbours would hear."

"Could this have been a robbery gone wrong?" asked Rocco. "We could do with knowing if there's anything missing."

"We need to search the house anyway. Find the names of any family members so that we can inform them. Also work colleagues; anything and everything in fact that will help us build a picture of this man's life. But this is no robbery, Rocco. The stabbing is one thing — that might have happened as the result of some altercation but not that." He nodded at the nail pinning the card to the doctor's face. "What is that, anyway? It's not like any playing card I've ever seen."

"It's a tarot card, Inspector," Julian informed him in that superior way of his. "They're used for divination purposes. That one in particular is rather interesting. It's one of the Major Arcana — 'the Tower', otherwise known as the bolt from the blue.

Calladine was astonished at the seriousness of Julian's tone. "You mean mumbo jumbo?"

"As you wish, Inspector. But as I said; this card is interesting. It has a number of different meanings, but to many, it symbolises failure, ruin and catastrophe."

"Neither Doctor Ahmed nor I would argue with you on that one."

"Perhaps the killer was trying to tell us something, Inspector. We should be open to all possibilities."

Calladine shook his head. He had no idea how such a clinical, logical guy as Julian Batho would know about stuff like this, but he didn't ask. He didn't fancy a lecture on the subject. Even so, it was intriguing in a rational individual like Julian.

Calladine looked back towards the front door and then went into the kitchen and sitting room to look at the windows.

"There's no sign of a break in. So whoever did this was either let in or had a key. The doctor knew him," he observed to Ruth. "Find out if he was expecting anyone — a visitor or even a patient. Look for a diary, laptop or something, and see if you can find his mobile phone. Perhaps he saw patients privately. Look around, see if you can find a consulting room. The house is certainly big enough. We need to know everything there is to know about the man. That thing on his face could be meaningful but it could also be nothing other than the killer having a laugh at our expense."

"It's weird though, sir. Perhaps we should have a look at the local fortune tellers — he might have a link to one of them," Rocco suggested.

"Okay, if you must," he told the young detective. "But don't waste too much time. It might be more use to find out if there's any CCTV in the street outside. Properties like these often have their own cameras. One of them might have caught something. Ruth!" She was talking to Doc Hoyle. "Will you get back to the nick and put what we've got on the incident board? Ask Imogen to find out what she can about Tariq Ahmed from the hospital, particularly regarding his family."

"Don't you want a lift back home, sir?"

"No, I'm going to the morgue with the doc. See what his preliminary findings turn up." He smiled.

He was back, well and truly back in harness once again. This case was everything he'd been missing. Languishing around the house with Lydia at his beck and call was one thing, but this was what he was really made for.

# CHAPTER 2

Calladine got himself a cup of coffee while Doc Hoyle and his assistant prepared the body. By the time the inspector entered the post-mortem room Tariq Ahmed was laid out on the table.

He'd never been squeamish; even as a rookie cop the post-mortem room had held no fears, but since the shooting that had changed. He couldn't help but picture his own body lying cold and still on the slab. He shuddered.

Tariq Ahmed was Asian and slight in build. He had a full head of greying black hair and the only obvious wounds were those to his back and right eye.

"It's as I said, Tom. He was stabbed in the back. Interesting angle though — I'll have to open him up to clarify but I'd say whoever did this was shorter than our victim." Calladine watched the doc poke at the air in an upward movement, demonstrating what he thought the deadly stroke might have looked like.

"He isn't particularly tall himself," Calladine noted. "So what are you saying?"

"Don't rule anyone out, that's all. This is a crime that could have been committed by either a man or a woman. With the element of surprise, no great strength would be needed."

"Or a youngster?"

At that the doc pulled a face. "Grim idea that one — but yes, I suppose so."

"Any signs of a struggle, Doc?"

"There are no abrasions or defensive wounds on his hands or arms. No knocks to the head or face, other than the one where he banged his head as he fell." He examined the body. "It looks like it was pretty clean to me. One stab to the back and it was all over."

"So he didn't see it coming. He was taken by surprise, and our killer chose the right area to aim for. Would that require any special knowledge, familiarity with anatomy for example?"

"Possibly. This is a cool customer and no mistake. But it could equally just have been a lucky blow."

"Lucky! God help the poor bloke on a bad day."

"Back for good, Tom? Recovered? Finally over what happened?"

"Yep, I rather think I am," he admitted with a smile. "I've had enough of sitting about feeling sorry for myself. Ruth tells me things are bad at the nick so they need me." He grinned.

"She's struggling with Long and his sidekick. Their methods are . . . shall we just say, an acquired taste."

"God knows what the powers that be were thinking putting Brad Long in charge," Calladine snorted. "Want their bloody heads looking at."

"Jones was a mess, and you weren't available, Tom," Hoyle reminded him.

"Wouldn't have wanted the job anyway. I'm getting to the point where I want to take on less, not more."

Hoyle gave him a doubtful look. Calladine sighed. He'd never explained the reasons why he'd not made DCI, and the Doc had never pried.

"You do know who this is, don't you, Tom?" He changed the subject.

"Some doctor from City Hospital."

"Not just some doctor — he's a consultant oncologist and one of the best in the north of England. This guy will be greatly missed by the profession as well as family and friends."

"Would he have enemies — within his field, I mean?"

"I wouldn't have thought so. He was very well thought of."

"Well, someone bore him a grudge, that's for sure."

"I'll do all the usual tests, confirm exactly how he died, and get back to you. I should have the full report some time tomorrow."

\* \* \*

"Guv! You're back," Imogen Goode exclaimed as Calladine walked into the main office, surprising them all. The blonde DC got up from her desk and, abandoning all protocol, threw her arms around him and kissed him on the cheek. "Sorry! I don't mean to be overfamiliar or anything." Her cheeks were pink with embarrassment. "But we haven't half missed you. I shouldn't have done that, should I?" Her cheeks flushed an even brighter shade of red.

Calladine chuckled and gently removed her arm from his shoulder. "Okay, Imogen, I get it and it's fine. No fuss — but a cuppa wouldn't go amiss."

"I'll get you one, sir, good and strong just as you like it."

He looked around the office — Joyce, the team's admin assistant caught his eye and nodded. "You look a lot better," she told him. "A lot better than you did in hospital when we visited."

"The rest has done me good."

He watched as she grabbed a pile of papers from her desk and made for the door — she was blushing slightly too. What was it with the women in this room? It was rumoured, mostly by Ruth, that Joyce carried something of a torch for him. Hopefully that uncomfortable bit of tittle-tattle would come to nothing. He'd no idea what he'd do if she suddenly found the courage to ask him out for a drink or something.

Imogen, Joyce, Rocco and Ruth — the same team with as yet no additions, so they'd still be stretched. He'd speak to Long — not that he expected an acting DCI to have much influence.

Ruth had made a start with the incident board. A photo of Tariq Ahmed and a tarot card — not the one from the scene; that was with Julian Batho. She had bought a pack on her way back to the station.

"There's a shop just off Leesdon High Street that sells them. In fact it sells all sorts of weird stuff: crystals, cards, incense and the like. I'm nipping back later for a chat. It's possible that our murderer bought the cards there."

"They're available online too don't forget — all different designs and quite cheap," Imogen piped up as she returned with Calladine's tea. Julian will tell us if it's new or old. It was difficult to make that out with all the blood on it," Ruth told them. "But if it was new, then it's worth a shot."

"Imogen, have you got anywhere with the staff at the city hospital?"

"Doctor Ahmed's secretary was not available when I rang and the medical team he worked with were in various clinics. So no, I didn't get anywhere."

"We should get down there. We need to speak to Doctor Ahmed's colleagues quickly," Calladine told Ruth as he sipped his tea.

"Hadn't you better check in with Long first?" she suggested with a smirk. "He's got Thorpe on the job don't forget."

She had a point. So where was Thorpe? Where had he got to with the case? Calladine left the main office and walked down the corridor to what was now DCI Long's office. The door was open and he could see DS Thorpe lolling in a chair with his feet up.

"You didn't stay long, Sergeant — get what you needed?"

"Nothing to get — wait for forensics then take another look." He shrugged and looked at Long, who was staring at Calladine quizzically.

"You back, Tom? Does that mean the doc's given you the all clear? You're not still on a sick note are you?"

He'd forgotten about that little bit of red tape. Now he'd have to get an appointment and waste yet more time.

"I'm seeing him in the morning," he lied. "He'll give me the all clear — I'm fine."

Calladine saw Long's expression lighten. He wouldn't care one way or the other. Sick note or no sick note, he'd just be glad to have someone else do the grafting.

"What are you up to?"

"We're looking into the Tariq Ahmed murder. Ruth and I are off to the city hospital, to meet with his colleagues. Get a feel for what the man was like."

"Thorpe — you going with them?" Long asked.

"I've still got work on the Prideau case to get through." Thorpe was chewing gum and had his hands in his pockets.

"Fine with me." Calladine was only too pleased to have him off his back.

"So you'll take this one on?" Long asked him.

"Yep. I'll keep you posted."

"Occupational Health will want a chat. Don't forget to sort things out with them. Like it or not, eventually I'll have to deal with the paperwork."

Occupational Health! Calladine usually did his best to stay away from that lot. What could they possibly know about the job he did and whether he was up to it or not. Office-bound pen pushers the lot of them.

"You set to go, Ruth?"

"Yes, sir," she answered reaching for her coat. "Rocco's been on, he's found some CCTV, so he's bringing it in. Want to wait around for him or what?"

"No — we'll see what he's got when we get back. Imogen, what do you know about the Prideau case?" He hadn't asked when Long mentioned it but if Thorpe was on the job then perhaps he should keep an eye out.

"We've got a missing child, sir: Isla Prideau. Thorpe took the case on. He did some initial investigations but got nowhere. I did some background on that one, but he didn't want to listen to my theories." She shrugged. "So I had no choice but to leave him to it."

"What theories?"

He watched as Imogen brought up some information on her screen. "There are two kids missing, sir — the Prideau girl from Hopecross and another one, Leah Cassidy from Oldston. I think the two are linked. Thorpe doesn't, and he wouldn't even look at what I'd got. Both girls are the same age, both just starting school and their mothers had social media accounts. They'd posted photos of the little girls online, both in their school uniforms, and within hours they were both missing. I thought that, and the fact that there's only eight miles between Hopecross and Oldston, too much of a coincidence."

"So do I. What about Long? Wasn't he interested?"

"He didn't seem to be. I think he's leaving it up to Thorpe."

Bloody idiot! Two kids missing and, effectively, no one was doing anything about it. Tariq Ahmed or not, Calladine would have to give it some consideration — and fast.

"Get all the stuff you've got on the case together and I'll take it and give it the once-over tonight," he told her. "We'd better go. You'll have to drive," he told Ruth. "I've not got mine — remember?"

"I suppose that means I'll be taking you home too. Deliver you safely back to Lydia once we're done."

The two detectives made their way out to the car park. Ruth had a smile on her face, Calladine noted. "Pleased to have me back then?"

"Well, you're a refreshing change from Thorpe. This new case — I couldn't have taken it on with him. Why he ever came into police work is a mystery. He does his level best to avoid doing anything constructive."

"So you've got me and a juicy case to get stuck into. Couldn't be better."

"Don't flatter yourself. Working with you has its down-side, believe me."

17

"You can cut the backchat, Sergeant."

"It's not backchat, it's the truth. It's no picnic, you know, sorting out your family problems. Not to mention your love life."

"It's not my fault. Things happen; people happen."

"Where you're concerned, don't they just!"

"Is that why I didn't see much of you while I was laid up?"

"No — too busy. Long's team has no idea. Take the missing children — all they've done is run around in circles. You see, one of the girls is from Oldston, so Long was only too happy to let them take the lead. Thankfully they've got some new DI there and he's good, so I'm told. Also I took a holiday — well, if you can call keeping watch on a peregrine falcon nest in central Manchester a holiday." She grinned.

"Each to their own. I wouldn't have thought birds like that would go for city life."

"Plenty of food. All those dopey pigeons."

He hadn't thought about it like that. But they were predators, and would go wherever the food was on tap. A bit like their child snatcher, if that's what he was. Social media had a lot to answer for. Calladine sighed. There'd been a missing girl on the last case he worked on before he was shot — Cassie Rigby. That had turned out okay. But this was different, this was two little girls.

\* \* \*

Once they were underway, with Ruth driving, he gave her a searching look. "You've changed," he declared. "And don't say it's my imagination because I know when things are different."

"It's the same me, Tom. Probably I look different because we've not worked together in a while."

"No it's not that, there's a change in you. You've grown your hair, and it's several shades lighter, and that skirt's rather short by your standards."

He'd never realised it before but Ruth had a really good pair of legs. The rest of her was shaping up rather well these days too.

"I've got a man in my life," she laughed. "And anyway, I've decided it's a good thing to make the most of myself."

"You two sorted out your differences?"

"More than that, we've decided to make a go of things. It took some doing though. I spent some time with the birding group and he went to see his parents in Whitby. The time apart did us good, made us both realise what's important. You see it wasn't Jake that was the problem back then, it was the commitment stuff that terrified me."

"Well, you look good on it — it suits you."

"A compliment, I'm honoured." She grinned. "Wish I could say something nice about the way you look too, boss, but to be truthful, you're still looking a bit rough. Not too much for you, this jumping straight back into the hot seat?"

"Charming. Been going to flattery school or what?" he joked. "But don't worry about me. I'm fine. This is just what I need."

"You've missed us, then — us and the cut and thrust of the job? I know we've all missed you."

"I've been living in a sort of limbo land. I wanted to come back but I got stuck in a rut. Life on the sofa, in front of the telly and having Lydia run herself stupid to keep me fed."

"I'm surprised you want to give that up — given how you feel about her."

"Lydia or not, I've still got to work. The bills and the boredom don't go away you know. I've decided to chalk what happened down to sheer bad luck and get on with things. But I'm still surprised I didn't see more of you. You kept your distance, you and the team."

"Well, it's difficult, isn't it? Lydia is still pressing and she's always on the hunt for a story," she explained. "If any of us said anything about work she'd be on it straight away and then there's the *other thing*. I could hardly talk about that — could I?"

"What other thing?"

"Pandora."

"What do you mean? Pandora who?"

"Don't play dumb with me. I'm talking about the *shock in the box* — the box I'm keeping for you, the one your mother left you, the one with your past in it."

He shut his eyes. Why now? Oh why did she have to bring that up now? He'd put it right out of his mind and as far as he was concerned, that's where it could stay. He hadn't been ready to deal with what he'd found out then and he was no nearer now. He sighed deeply. Life had once been so simple. He used to know exactly who he was, where he'd come from, who his family members were. He used to have a history, with names and faces. Now all he had was a gaping hole where his mother should have been. Well, not a hole exactly, there was a name — Eve Walker.

"I know we've not talked much these last few weeks, since that day — you know, the day you got shot, but that's not because I didn't want to. I didn't know where to start. But don't think that I've forgotten, because I've been dying to ask. Have you done anything about finding her, your birth mother?"

Of course he bloody hadn't. He'd been in no fit state. When his mother had died she'd left him a few hundred quid and the revelation that he was the product of an affair his father had had fifty-two years ago with some woman he'd never heard of.

"I haven't even told my daughter yet, and certainly not Lydia." He watched her expression change — from incredulity that he could keep something so big to himself, to disappointment.

"Why not? I'd have thought your Zoe had a right to know. She is your daughter. This affects her too," she told him sharply.

"She doesn't need to know anything, not until I decide. Come on — how do I tell her that her granny was a fake?

That her real granny is some woman I don't even know, that I've never even met? What's she going to think about my dad? Come to think about it what am I supposed to think about him? So don't you go saying anything either."

"She wasn't a fake. Freda Calladine was your mother; she brought you up, and that made her Zoe's gran. Despite all the bad feelings you have, you've got to be curious, surely?"

"Look, for now the box stays with you, away from prying eyes, and I don't want to take things any further — not just yet."

"But she's your mother — well, your birth mother. For all you know, this Eve Walker might still live locally, you might even know her already!"

"If I drag all that up it'll have repercussions. Lydia only stays with me because Fallon's my cousin. A cousin on Freda's side, I might remind you — my pretend mother," he emphasised with annoyance. "If she finds out he's not — then I doubt she'd be so keen."

"Is she really that shallow? You need to make your mind up. Do you want rid of Fallon, and to get your career back on track, or Lydia?"

"You did try to warn me — how shallow she is, weeks ago, remember?"

"Fallon's in prison awaiting trial. It can't matter to her now what he is to you."

"That's where you're wrong, because it does matter. She's still after a story and Fallon has agreed to see her, to talk. So for the time being I'd prefer to keep things as they are."

"I'd have thought you'd be dead keen to tell the world Fallon's no kin of yours. He was one of Manchester's biggest crime barons. You should be jumping for joy. There are times when I really don't understand you, Tom Calladine!"

"Yes, alright, don't rub it in. Fact is I like having Lydia around, so I don't want the boat rocking — not yet."

"You're making a mistake."

"Well, it's my mistake to make, so leave it."

"You know, you can be a most irritating man when you choose to be. Anyway — it's too late."

"Too late for what?"

"To leave it. I've already looked her up."

Ruth hunched over the steering wheel waiting for his angry reaction, but there wasn't one.

# CHAPTER 3

After an irritating five minutes of silent crawling around the hospital car park, Ruth eventually found a space. Calladine had said nothing and that wasn't good. He was most likely seething inside because of what she'd done, and any second she'd get a tongue-lashing. They sat for a moment, both facing forward.

"So," he said at last. "What did you find out?"

So that was his game. Feign lack of interest. Let her do all the donkey work and then sit back and get the information anyway.

She looked at him. His voice had been surprisingly even, and his expression had hardly changed.

"You're not angry, then?" She was incredulous. "I've been dreading telling you, but I was too curious not to do something."

"Too bloody nosy, you mean. I can't pretend, Ruth. I might not show it but I'm damned annoyed."

Here it comes. He might look okay but he was actually sitting there quietly seething.

"I don't see why. She's your mother for goodness sake. You're just not brave enough to do anything about it yourself."

"I wanted it left for a reason." He ran his hand through his short hair. "This whole thing will cause too much upset. I was even considering just letting it lie, doing nothing — ever."

Ruth shook her head. She didn't understand his attitude, why this should upset him so much. His face was ashen. Had she gone too far? Taken liberties? No — he needed to do this; otherwise it would eat a hole in him.

"Don't be such a wimp," she retorted. "That idea is ludicrous. You need to do this, find her, speak to her and get her side of things. Don't you want to know why she gave you up, what she's like?"

"No, not really. She gave me away because she didn't want me, that much is obvious. My dad will have made it easy for her. So she jumped at the chance to get her life back."

"Bollocks! It'll be nothing like that. You're scared, Tom Calladine, and I'm disappointed in you."

Ruth Bayliss got out of the car, swung her bag over her shoulder and walked off towards the main entrance of the hospital.

"Wait up! I've been injured, remember?"

"Coward!" she threw back at him.

"Mind your cheek, Sergeant. I'm still your boss — remember that."

Ruth flashed him one of her unimpressed looks, tossed back her hair and carried on, as he lagged behind her.

"Suits you!" he shouted after her. "The change of look I mean."

Ruth smiled to herself. He'd come round. He wasn't stupid, he knew she was right.

"Okay — I give in. You're going to tell me — so later. We'll get a coffee and you can give me the lowdown," he panted, catching her up. "No good arguing — you're going to get your own way, so why fight it?"

Ruth had known she'd win him round. He couldn't kid her. Deep down he was every bit as curious about Eve Walker as she was. How could he not be? He was a detective and the woman was his mother.

Ruth gave him a conspiratorial smile as she presented her badge to the woman in the reception area and asked to see Doctor Ahmed's secretary.

\* \* \*

Celia Downs was middle-aged, wore her hair in a tight bun on the top of her head and had round-framed glasses perched on the bridge of her nose. She looked older than she probably was, and she didn't smile much either.

"DI Calladine and DS Bayliss from Leesworth CID." Calladine introduced them. "I'm not sure if you are aware but Doctor Ahmed was found dead earlier today. Murdered in his own home."

Her distinctly pinched expression didn't change. She simply moved her birdlike eyes from Ruth to Calladine.

"Yes, I know. It's been on the news. So what are you doing about it?"

Calladine knew that there'd been no press release yet, and he wondered how they had got hold of the story so fast.

"We're investigating, Mrs Downs, that's what we're doing. First we need to get a feel for what the doctor was like. I need to know about his family, his friends, if there was anybody giving him a hard time. In short, I need as much information as you can give me about him."

"It's Ms," she corrected.

Now why didn't that surprise him?

"He didn't have any family. He never married, had no children and he was an only child, I believe. He had an elderly mother in Pakistan, but I imagine she's dead by now."

"Had anyone given him any grief recently? Were there any arguments or other altercations with staff or patients? Did the doctor have any enemies that you know of?

"No, of course not." She frowned at them. "Doctor Ahmed was an eminent oncologist, first class in his field. He'll be greatly missed by the profession."

"An all-round nice guy then?" Ruth chipped in.

"Nice . . ." Celia Downs thought for a moment then shook her head. "No, I don't think so — that's not the adjective I'd use to describe him. He might not have had enemies, but Doctor Ahmed wasn't easy to get on with, not easy at all. He was a hard man. He could deliver the worst possible news to his patients without any emotion at all. The man was completely lacking in empathy, you see."

"And there'd be a lot of bad news, I take it?" Calladine surmised.

"Greater Manchester has a large number of cancer patients and the fact of the matter is that they don't get diagnosed soon enough and so they die," she told him soberly. "Doctor Ahmed worked hard, he did what he could — whatever was possible for all his patients, but, I'm afraid, the personal touch was absent."

"Any of his patients take the bad news particularly hard lately?" Ruth asked.

"As his secretary, it's difficult to say. You'll need to talk to his clinical staff."

"I intend to," Calladine confirmed. "Back to the question about friends; as his secretary you must have had to arrange things for him from time to time. He had no wife to do it."

"He had little social life to speak of, Inspector. Drinks at Christmas with the staff, and then only the one, and I've no idea about anything else."

"Are you sure there is no one in his circle who might be jealous of the doctor, bear a grudge and act on it?"

"I can't answer that. I've no idea what goes on in people's heads. The people Doctor Ahmed met were mostly patients. They were very sick, Inspector. Even if they didn't like him much, it's unlikely they'd have the energy or the will to do much about it."

"Okay, then, clinical staff — can you arrange for us to talk to them?"

"Certainly — you need Doctors Hurst and Hussain. Both are on the wards or in theatre at present. If you leave your card I'll get them to come in and see you . . . In my opinion, Inspector, whoever did this will be someone nearer to home. I doubt it will turn out to have anything to do with this hospital."

* * *

Albert North wasn't very good on his feet these days. But the dog needed walking and that waster of a nephew of his hadn't shown his face all day. It wasn't late, just gone six and ordinarily he'd be making his way to the pub about now for a pint and a chinwag with his mates. Now he'd have to forgo that and take the damn dog out himself. He'd give Jayden a clip around the ear when he did eventually turn up. Inconsiderate little bastard.

He grunted at the animal and reached up for its lead, taking it down from a coat hook. He'd walk him over the common and make it back before it got too dark. Not that Albert North was afraid of the dark — Albert North wasn't afraid of anything. Time was when most of the folk living around here — on the Hobfield Estate — were afraid of him. He'd been the man — the man with drugs to sell, and the man you didn't cross. He sighed wearily. That was a lifetime ago, and those passing years hadn't gone easy on him.

These days he was old and infirm. He'd had a stroke and it had left him unsteady. He didn't like to stray too far from his flat — the pub, the post office and occasionally the doctors and that was about it. Rarely did he venture out to walk the dog — that was supposed to be Jayden's job.

He pulled his stocky frame into his coat and scarf and whistled for the mutt. The beast was old like him and wouldn't give him any trouble. He took the lift down to the ground floor and left the block by the side door. There was nobody about, too bloody cold.

It took him about ten minutes to shuffle his way onto the common. He'd keep to the perimeter, he didn't want to stumble and do himself an injury. It was icy. He hated nights like this, cold and dark. He was shivering, the wind bit deep into his bones and his legs were stiff. Bloody Jayden making promises he couldn't keep.

He hadn't been out long but he was already breathless and his knee hurt. He was down for a new one but he'd probably be dead before the NHS called him in. He lowered his heavy frame onto a bench by some trees and let the dog off his lead for a while. He leaned back and closed his eyes. God it was freezing — far too cold for him. He rubbed his gloved hands together and hunkered down into his coat. He'd give the dog five minutes or so and then it was back to his warm flat.

"You've not seen a cat?" A female voice interrupted his thoughts. "This cat."

The woman shoved a piece of paper in front of his nose and waved it at him. "I've looked everywhere. The poor thing's never done anything like this before. I've been searching for Mitzie all week but there's no sign."

Who calls their cat 'Mitzie'? Albert wondered. He didn't even bother to look up at her but shuffled up so she could sit down.

"Wrong glasses on," was his excuse for not examining the piece of paper she was still wafting about. "Dog person myself, don't like cats. Smelly things." He was mumbling through the scarf wrapped around his face.

"Not my Mitzie. She's a beautiful cat, won prizes and everything," she protested, flopping down beside him. "I've been out for ages, I'm beginning to think I'll never find her," she moaned.

Albert grunted at this — he wasn't impressed, cats were dreadful creatures. He inhaled the cold air. There was a smell, one he recognised — whiskey. The woman had pulled a flask from her bag and was pouring the hot alcohol into a beaker.

* * *

The cat talk was getting Harriet nowhere. Even after all this time, at the very least she'd expected him to recognise her voice. But it was obvious he had no idea who she was, and that was disappointing because she wanted him to know. She wanted him afraid, and to know why his life was going to end very soon — horrifically.

"You don't remember me, do you?" Harriet was angry again. These days she lost control easily. The rage seemed to boil permanently within her. It had the upper hand and it made her do things. But it also gave her an edge, the energy to see things through.

His indifference made her want to strike him. She had hated this man for as long as she could remember so how could he not know her? She couldn't do this anonymously; he had to understand, feel the fear. He must be made to remember what he'd done. Then he would die, and she'd be satisfied. This was too important for her to continue with the charade about the cat.

She watched him shrug. He wasn't interested. "If you knew who I was and what I was going to do, then you wouldn't sit there so calmly."

But her words were going over his head — they obviously meant nothing to him. Harriet could see that in his eyes she was nothing but a batty old woman. Right now he was far more interested in keeping out the cold than listening to what she had to say.

"We've met before, and I swore then that I'd get even. I'm surprised you've no memory of it. It was quite an occasion — the courtroom. Remember now?

But Albert simply grunted. He wasn't even listening.

"I expended a lot of hate and venom that day." She sniffed, and took a swig of whiskey. "You must remember that day in court when you were had up for killing my Jimmy."

At that Albert coughed and stamped his feet on the hard ground against the cold.

Still nothing — not even a hint of remorse. The man deserved to die.

"Hot toddy." She surprised him by holding out the flask. "Very strong, just how I like it. When I'm out like this I need something to keep out the cold."

Now she had his attention. She couldn't afford to bungle this and she wanted him distracted for the next bit.

She handed him the beaker and watched Albert grasp it gratefully in his gloved hands and take a sip. He swallowed the remainder in one gulp — she had plenty left in that flask of hers.

"He'd have been in his thirties now, my Jimmy," she droned on. "You robbed me of that. You robbed me of him and of grandchildren too, probably. You sit there all quiet and easy, and I bet you've got family, haven't you?"

Albert nodded.

Harriet guessed he'd be racking his brain, but was he any the wiser?

"You alright, love?" he asked. "You're not from that care home at the end of the road?"

So he thought she was demented — she'd show him!

"Jimmy Finch," she said sharply. "You must recall him — dark haired, skinny lad. Ran drugs for you on the Hobfield for long enough."

As she spoke her son's name she saw the first spark of recognition on Albert's face. That name rang a bell. If there was any justice he should be feeling the first shivers of terror snake down his spine.

"You had him done away with. You had him beaten to a pulp and dumped in the underpass by the dual carriageway. You and your thugs left him unconscious on a pile of rotting cardboard."

"Not me, love," he lied, his voice a mere rasp. "No way. You can't pin that on me."

"Oh, I know that — I tried back then and got nowhere. But it was you, Albert North. I know it was. You were the big man on the estate, the man who doled out the punishments. You beat him with a bat, the police said. Then you left him unconscious, bleeding heavily, and at the mercy of a pack of feral kids who set him alight."

"Not my fault, then. The kids did him, not me at all."

His head was bent — Harriet watched him inhale the steam that floated upwards from the beaker. He was using it to warm his face. She'd warm him alright! She fumbled in her bag again.

She got up from the bench and moved behind him. He didn't even turn to look at what she was up to — why should he? In his eyes she'd lost it. He saw her as a stupid old woman with a mad idea. out looking for her cat. How wrong he was.

Harriet unscrewed the cap from the petrol can she'd brought with her. Albert sat there helpless, unsuspecting — just like her Jimmy had been. Her rage was back. North deserved everything that was coming to him. She shook the contents wildly over Albert's head and then threw the can to the ground.

He was old and Harriet knew he wouldn't be quick enough to save himself. She saw the liquid run in rivulets down the side of his face and soak into his clothes. The strong vapours replaced the smell of whiskey in the air around them, making her feel sick. He swore. Harriet took a step back. His hands were clutching frantically at his petrol-sodden scarf. But it was too late.

She was shrieking at him. He was shouting, begging — he'd do anything, promise anything to stop this. Then she saw the look of horror on his face. He'd heard the sound of the striking match.

Harriet smiled. "That is for my Jimmy, you bastard!" Those were the last words Albert North ever heard.

Harriet dropped the match onto his scarf. He was too slow to react. A heartbeat later he had become a blazing torch — a human beacon lighting up the dark night.

Harriet stood well back and watched. She watched his skin shrivel and then appear to literally melt from his flesh. She waited until he ceased to scream, until he was unrecognisable

31

— his head nothing but a blackened, charred mess. His lower body wasn't too badly burned though, and no doubt the police would rifle through his clothing in an effort to find out who he was. With that thought in mind, she took a tarot card from her bag and placed it in his coat pocket.

The Devil — perfect for a man like Albert North.

# CHAPTER 4

*Wednesday*

Lydia was poking him in the ribs. "For heaven's sake, Tom, your mobile's been ringing on and off for the last ten minutes. Do something about it or it's going through the window," she hissed at him.

He prised his eyes open. "What time is it?"

"Some unearthly hour. If this is what it's like when you're working then you'll have to sleep in the spare room."

"I thought this was my house," he said, rubbing his stubbly face. "So shouldn't that be you in the spare room?"

"Come on, Detective, you don't really mean that, do you?" She ran her hand provocatively over his naked chest down to his navel. "You'd be far too lonely," she said, slapping his belly.

Minx she might be, but she was right; he would be lonely without her and not just in bed either. Calladine picked up his mobile from the table — Ruth. What now? "We've got another one, sir," she said at once. "It's not good. Another feast of horror for the eyes and I'm not kidding you. I'm on the common, near the small copse of trees opposite the bus

33

stop. You need to get down here fast. You need to see this because we need to get the body moved quickly."

"Another one?" His brain wasn't functioning on all cylinders yet.

"Another tarot card murder."

"So that's what we're calling them now?"

"It's what the press will call it if we don't get our act together." The phone went dead.

"Got to go," he told Lydia as he jumped out of bed. "Nasty case shaping up — could be gone all day."

"You haven't forgotten I'm seeing your cousin later? Visiting him in Strangeways?"

"No," he lied. "But why you're still chasing after that thug is beyond me."

"Because he has a story to tell, Tom, and he's going to tell it to me — exclusively. And when he does it'll blast my career to the sky," she enthused, rolling onto her back and stretching out her long limbs.

"Waste of time. He's using you. He'll have an angle, take my word for it."

"Don't care," she sniffed. "I need this, and I won't be put off."

"The man tried to kill me."

"And I saved you, so don't cross me on this. It won't go down well."

Once Calladine had showered and dressed, he went back into the bedroom and kissed her mouth gently. She'd gone back to sleep.

* * *

The sun was just rising as he arrived at Leesdon Common. He parked by the road and walked towards the taped-off area. The unmistakable smell of burnt flesh hung in the air. He shivered. Poor bugger, whoever he'd been. Ruth and Rocco were on the scene and had things organised.

"Sir!" Rocco shouted to him. "Think we've got an ID."

Calladine nodded a greeting to the young DC, but it was the sight of Albert North's body, still seated on the bench, that caught his full attention. His lower body and clothing looked practically intact but the upper half was a mess. How could anyone ID that?

"He must have been walking his dog," Rocco explained. "Eventually it took itself off home and his nephew," he said, nodding at the corpse, "came looking for him. He's Albert North, lived on the Hobfield."

Calladine knew North alright, and where he had lived. He'd spent a great deal of his time as a rookie cop chasing after the reprobate. He'd been a bad lot back then and from the look of him, he was still upsetting people today.

"Can the nephew say for sure that this is North?" he asked doubtfully.

"He recognises the clothing, what's left of it, and the dog certainly knew him. Don't think I've ever seen a dog more distraught."

"How long ago?" Calladine asked, turning to Doc Hoyle who was with the ambulance people.

"Last night, I'd say."

"So what links it to the other case?"

"This, Inspector." Julian Batho showed him the tarot card they had found in Albert's pocket, now secured in an evidence bag. "We've got an empty fuel can too. I'll get it back to the lab and see what's what. I'll be in touch."

Calladine sighed. He didn't know what to make of this. Apart from the cards, there was nothing obvious to link the cases at all. Different method and the men were poles apart socially. So what did they have in common?

The bad feeling was back — the one he got when things were worse than he'd realised and they were up against it. He beckoned Ruth over to join him. She'd been talking to the nephew. He saw her pat his arm comfortingly and pass him over to the ambulance crew who were waiting to take North's body to the morgue.

"Looks like we've got a serial killer, Ruth," Calladine told her quietly. "We need to do some digging, but I can't see what could possibly link North to Ahmed." He shuddered. "I just hope our killer isn't choosing people at random — that's all we need," he said, stamping his feet up and down against the cold.

"Albert lived very quietly according to his nephew."

"He did recently. But not when I knew him. The man was a right villain back in the day."

"According to his nephew he couldn't get about much anymore due to a stroke he had a while ago. He wasn't a well man. He was breathless most of the time and had a failing heart. This wasn't part of his usual routine — walking his dog on the common, I mean."

"Perhaps he wasn't the target, then. Who was it usually took the dog out?"

"Jayden — his nephew over there."

He didn't look more than twenty. This must be a nightmare for him, seeing his uncle like this. Calladine wondered if he knew about North's past — the things he'd done, the trouble and misery he'd caused. "We'll look at him closely too, in that case. But even if the victim's a case of mistaken identity, I still don't see where the tie-up is."

"It could be anything — drugs, the hospital or something else. North was a patient and Ahmed a doctor. That could be something. I'll check it out — see what clinics North attended," said Ruth.

"It looks to me like he was doused in a flammable liquid and set alight. Whatever was in that can most likely," Doc Hoyle offered. "Most of the heat seems to have been at the neck area and his head. That was down to the thick scarf he was wearing. Soaked up most of the accelerant and then burned good and hot."

Calladine winced. The old man wouldn't have been able to help himself — it'd all have happened too quickly. "Get the body back," he told Hoyle. "I'll come and see you later once I've briefed the team."

"I think most of your team are here, aren't they, Tom? There's only DC Goode missing."

True. It was a measure of how short-handed they were. Calladine looked around. There was no sign of Thorpe, and he was grateful for that.

* * *

"All we can say for now is that the two men were murdered, but everything about those murders is different. Despite the different methods used we're still looking for only one killer. The reason? Because one of these was left at the scene of both," Calladine told the team, pointing to the two tarot cards pinned to the incident board. "I can't even begin to understand what they mean but we'll find someone who does and they may be able to cast some light. That shop in town," he said to Ruth. "The one you bought the new cards from — perhaps they can enlighten us."

"I'll go back and ask," she nodded, making a note.

"We'll both go," he decided. Suddenly the fact of the cards had become important. "This is different from other multiple killings we've dealt with. For a start we're used to killers using a single method of dispatch. Serial killers have a tried and tested way of operating that they've perfected over time. What's baffling about this is the different methods."

He rubbed the back of his head and stood away from the board. "Anyone have any ideas?"

"Could we have two killers — each using their own methods but each with a common purpose — operating together?" Imogen offered.

Calladine nodded. She might have a point, but he thought it was unlikely. The tarot card left at both crime scenes told him another story.

"If it is one killer then perhaps they're just starting out," Rocco suggested. "Perhaps they haven't found their particular method yet."

"It doesn't work like that, Rocco," Calladine told him. "No — I'm certain we're looking for one person who knew them both."

"But the doctor and North lived in entirely different social circumstances. So who'd know them both?" Rocco asked.

"Albert North and Doctor Ahmed can't possibly be linked," Imogen argued. "I doubt they have anyone or anything in common. North was from the Hobfield and the doctor from the posh part of Leesworth. North was retired and the doctor at the hospital all day, every day."

"The link is the killer. He or she could be a tradesman, someone delivering groceries, the list is endless once you think about it," Calladine pointed out. "We're going to have to dig, because the link is there. Somewhere. We've got to find it because there's no guarantee that this is the last one."

"You're expecting more?" Imogen asked.

"We've no way of knowing, but it looks to me like someone's on a mission."

Brad Long entered the incident room. He nodded to the team and handed Calladine a piece of paper. "Julian sent this up. He reckons you need to look at the summary of his findings right away."

"How's Thorpe doing with the case of the missing child?"

"He's following a lead but it's a wild goose chase if you ask me. The child could be anywhere — it's been days."

"Shouldn't we be doing more?"

"With what? With who?" Long puffed out his fat cheeks. "We're stretched to the limit as it is. Anyway I've given Oldston the heads up, and asked them to look at ours in tandem with their Cassidy case. That new guy they've got, DI Greco, is looking at it now."

"The Prideau girl disappeared on our patch. It should be down to us to find her."

"We can't afford to be that idealistic, Tom. I wish we could, but we just don't have the resources."

Calladine sighed discontentedly and looked at what Julian had sent him. He scanned the single sheet of A4 stamped 'urgent' in red ink.

"This backs up my theory that we're looking for one killer," he told the team.

"So it has to be someone who knew both Albert North and Doctor Ahmed," Rocco reiterated.

"Tariq Ahmed was a doctor. They see all sorts at the hospital," Imogen reasoned. "So our killer could be from the Hobfield and also have had some beef with the doctor."

"But why now? What is it that's prompted these killings?" It was a puzzler and Calladine's brain was out of practice. He'd just have to work on it.

"According to Julian's preliminary report," he told the team, "hairs were found on both Doctor Ahmed and Albert North's clothing — synthetic hairs, like those you get in a cheap wig. So if there were any doubts before, I think this dispels them. We're definitely looking for a solo killer."

"What colour?" Ruth asked.

"Grey and curly."

"Like an elderly woman's hair, sir — the sort of style that still requires rollers and a hairdryer at the salon."

"If you say so, Sergeant."

But she was right. When he thought back to when his mother was in the care home he could recall all the old dears having more or less the same style, and that just about summed it up — grey and curly.

"Then this could be someone in disguise, pretending to be elderly."

"Pretending to be an elderly woman," Ruth corrected him. "But why? What would that achieve?"

"Trust perhaps," he replied. "Who would be frightened of an old woman?"

Doc Hoyle had said the killer was small. Was their killer, in fact, a woman?

"Rocco, did you get that CCTV from the neighbour's house?"

"Yes, sir — I've got it set up ready to go. It's from a house three doors down from the doctor's. They have two cameras and one faces the drive and catches the footpath. It'll only be a snippet, if that, but given what we know about the hair now, it's worth a shot."

Calladine was hoping that even a stray shot of their killer would solve the gender question. "Will you get that sorted, Rocco? Get stills of everyone who passed that driveway after nine o'clock Monday night."

"Imogen — dig around a bit, will you? Dig around in Doctor Ahmed's past and see what you can find. We'll leave his patients until later — look at personal stuff first."

This wasn't going to be easy; they were a man down and Thorpe was useless.

"Ruth, we'd better go see the fortune teller now." He rolled his eyes.

"You shouldn't scoff," she warned.

"I'm not scoffing, just dubious," he corrected her. "First the shop, and then we need to do something about the doctor's patients. We're going to have to go through them all."

"The hospital won't like it, sir. We'll need special permission, the lot."

"We'll get a warrant. Whatever it takes but we'll leave it until it becomes vital," he decided.

# CHAPTER 5

As Harriet Finch opened her eyes the full horror of what she'd done struck her like a thunderclap. The old Harriet was back — the one who knew full well that her recent actions had been horribly wrong. The Harriet with the conscience was on her case, urging her to stop before things got out of hand.

Too late for that — she'd killed two men in as many days. What in hell's name had possessed her?

Stupid question. She knew very well. A woman she barely recognised was responsible, a version of Harriet Finch who would eventually take over her mind completely. This new version was hell bent on revenge. She was a woman on a mission, but what was worse, she was pressed for time.

She lay in bed and stared at the ceiling. She was evil, a murderer. Could she be stopped? No, not now; it was far too late.

The panic went to her stomach like a blow from a heavy fist. She coughed violently, made a dash to the bathroom and vomited down the toilet.

*Calm down, you're safe* — the new Harriet reassured. But was she? Harriet was living in a sort of bubble, but one that could burst at any time. When it did, she'd be carted off to

41

prison. The ignominy; the shame. What was left of her family would never cope with it.

She crawled back to her bed and sat on the edge, exhausted, her body shaking. *You have to finish this*, the cold hard voice told her. *You promised and you owe it to those you love.*

"Loved," Harriet corrected out loud. "They're nearly all gone, and that's the whole point." She sighed wearily. "That's what you want, isn't it? Revenge, chaos and more misery."

She heard laughter in her head. The voice was taunting her. This wasn't who she was. Harriet Finch wasn't a killer — not the old Harriet Finch anyway. It was the cancer that had changed her. The cancer had taken on a personality, and one which had nothing but raw intent. It demanded and pushed, and Harriet could refuse it nothing. She was powerless against its energy, its will.

The voice was insidious; it warned her that she had to act now. She must be quick and avenge those she'd loved. She was haunted by the faces of people long dead. They cried out to her in her dreams and in her head when she was awake, as they joined the voice. They too wanted vengeance, and like it or not, they'd made her their vehicle.

She had to take control if she was to see this through to the end. And it must start now, today. Harriet, the new Harriet, had to get on with it. She might be at death's door herself, but there were still things to do. And the voice kept telling her that time was running out. Any day now she might become bedridden and her task would remain unfinished. If she was going to complete this, then she had to get on with things.

*Gordon Lessing* — *he's the next one*, the voice whispered. *You know how evil he is, you know the truth about him. He finished your poor sister, Sybil. But it wasn't just Sybil, was it? The children, Harriet. You know, you've suspected all along, and still you're silent. Your silence is deafening! You know what he's done and you know that he won't stop. So why in all these years have you never spoken out? That's bad Harriet, very bad. Think of the misery he's given all those families, think of the children . . . But you can put that right now, can't you?*

42

Yes, she could, and Sybil would want that. Suddenly she understood. She knew what to do, but she'd have to plan carefully. It had to be a befitting end for the cruel bastard. It had to be something satisfying to watch, after what he'd done to those children and to Sybil.

Sybil. Her poor dead sister. She sobbed and dabbed her eyes. She never used to cry like this but these days she couldn't help it. Everything seemed so sad, so pointless. Sybil had never been able to stand up for herself, so she never had a chance against that pig of a man. Lessing was a bully, a controlling wicked bully. To everyone who knew them as a couple he gave the impression of being a good, caring provider. But it was a sham.

He pretended to be the successful businessman, always boasting about his haulage company and how it gave his family a very good living. But he only had two lorries and a van, and the lorries were run into the ground and spent most of the time parked up. So whatever he did, he'd have to do using the van. It had black paintwork and dark tinted windows. Harriet shuddered. He used it for watching the children. He'd park near a school; pretend he was waiting for one of his own, and watch. What he did then was something she didn't want to think about. He must be passing the information on to someone. She'd seen the headlines in the paper recently. She knew that two local girls were missing. He didn't fool her, not for a second. He didn't earn his money by transporting goods across Europe. It was the children.

He was involved with a group of eastern Europeans who were people trafficking — children trafficking to be precise. Sybil had suspected and she'd confided in Harriet. Back then the idea had seemed preposterous. Gordon was a steady, safe sort of man. How wrong she was.

Harriet didn't want to think about it anymore. It was too terrible. Lessing's job was to source them. It was the devil's work. He was part of a trade so wicked he deserved all he was going to get.

But dealing with Lessing would mean going out into the world again and that made her nervous. If she wanted to see him, it would have to be in the daytime. There was always the chance that Jane, his daughter and her niece, would be there in the evening. Where possible, she tried to manage everything during the hours of darkness. Daylight was not flattering. She looked terrible — like death itself, in fact.

However, one way or another Harriet would have to conceal the ravages of her illness, cover them up behind makeup and a wig. Chemotherapy had robbed her of both her looks and her hair. She'd wear the titian one. It was nearest to what her old hair colour had been.

The voice purred, quietly at last, happy with the plan: *He has a cellar, Harriet, everything you need is down there.*

Was it? Why there? She couldn't think; was she missing something?

Harriet looked at her reflection — the makeup helped, but not much. The wig looked garish against her sickly pallor. She screamed in frustration and threw the thing across the bedroom floor.

*That's it, girl*, the voice encouraged. She was hardly a girl — she was fifty-five and terminal. Her illness had stolen her energy and her looks. All she had left, all that was keeping her going, was the voice with its burning, all-consuming need for revenge.

If she didn't get caught this time then it was back to the treatment. But would she make it? Harriet couldn't understand why she was still at liberty. She was no expert, and she'd killed two people with no repercussions — not even a visit from the police. Well, not yet anyway. But it had made her nervous. Every phone call and every knock on the door made her sick with worry.

* * *

"Long didn't hang around, did he?" said Ruth.

"You don't really want that man nosing into everything we do, do you, Sergeant?" Calladine replied.

"That's not the point. He knows we're short on the team. He could have offered to help. I've no idea what he finds to do in that office of his all day."

"He'll have some time-wasting occupation to fill the hours, Ruth — believe me. Who was he on about? Who is DI Greco?"

"Well, apparently he's quite something," she told him conspiratorially. "He's some hotshot detective new to the area and stirring things up at Oldston nick from all accounts. He sounds okay."

"Have you met him?"

"I've not had that pleasure yet but I'm told he's young. Young, fit and from the south of England somewhere."

"Calm down, Sergeant, you're spoken for, remember?" he said, pulling a face. "How come Oldston get him and yet it's us that are short-handed? It makes no sense to me."

"It doesn't have to, sir. You know what they're like, the bigwigs, law unto themselves."

"Imogen should contact him — tell him her theories. Her research, what she's put together, it all sounds very plausible to me. She's put the work in — she should be allowed to help."

"I could speak to him and suggest it," Ruth said, turning into the High Street. "But she might find him hard going."

"What d'you mean?"

"He might be good, but there have been rumblings. One or two have said that DI Greco is just a little too picky for their liking. In fact one of the sergeants at Oldston told me that he thinks the new DI has some sort of condition. You know — like OCD. Apparently he's ultra-neat — always tidying things up, that sort of thing."

"So he's a nutter?"

"No," she protested, "he's neat, overly finicky if that's possible, and he likes to go over and over stuff before he makes up his mind. He's also a bit of a loner. He does have a good clear-up rate though."

"In that case I'm glad we haven't got him. You were right: he does sound like hard work."

"Don't get too happy. We could still get him — there is the DCI position at our nick going begging, remember?"

"There'll be a free parking space by the library; the shop is just around the corner," Calladine advised, ignoring her comment. "Is she scary?"

"Don't be daft, sir. She runs a shop, not a coven, and she's nice. I'm sure she'll help if she can."

\* \* \*

The shop was called *Starshine*. It was small, packed with all sorts of weird stuff Calladine didn't recognise, but it smelled divine. The detective inhaled deeply.

"The smell is jasmine — from the incense." The owner's laugh was a gentle melodic sound that made his nerve ends tingle.

"Relaxing, isn't it? You should try some at home, Inspector." And her bright blue eyes twinkled with amusement.

Calladine, who had just been about to proffer his badge, retracted his hand from his pocket, puzzled. "How do you know I'm police?"

"Because I live locally and I've seen you about," she told him. "It's not magic, it's just local knowledge." There was more twinkling of those incredible eyes.

So she'd noticed him. Calladine wasn't sure if he should be flattered or not. Did he really need another woman noticing him? But then again she was a very attractive woman. She looked to be in her mid-forties, tall with a full voluptuous figure, long sable-coloured hair and the bluest eyes he'd ever seen. Calladine stood, unable to do anything but stare at her for a good few seconds.

There was something mesmerising about her — not just the looks, it was the whole package. Her mode of dress was what he'd describe as 'bohemian,' or was it simply aging hippy? He shook himself — what on earth was going on? He'd only just clapped eyes on the woman and he was transfixed. There was Lydia at home and, although he'd never put it to the test, he had her down as being rather jealous.

"Amaris Dean." She gave him that dazzling smile again.

"Amaris?" He repeated the name almost in a whisper, still puzzled. He'd never heard the name before.

"Moon child — it's my Wicca name."

More stuff he didn't understand. He'd have to let it go; he certainly didn't have the time to get dragged in. Something told him this woman was dangerous. And not because she might possess some weird occult power, but because she might play havoc with his libido!

"Can you help us with these?" He cleared his throat and tried to get his mind back on track as he pulled the cards from his coat pocket.

"Ah! From the pack you bought here." She smiled at Ruth.

"You have two very powerful cards there, Inspector."

"We need your help and your knowledge or we wouldn't be disclosing this," he explained. "Our case could be destroyed if the press got wind of it. So I need your reassurance that this will go no further."

"You have it, Inspector. Whatever you tell me will not leave this shop."

There was something about the way she said it that made Calladine believe her at once. He instinctively felt that this was a woman he could trust.

"Both these cards were found at murder scenes — this at the first," he said holding out the Tower, "and this at the second. I need some help to understand what they mean."

She came closer. Calladine was aware of her scent; it was heady like the incense. Part of him was praying she wouldn't come too close — he was already sweating.

"The problem is that people tend to take the images literally."

Her voice had depth. Sexy. Calladine immediately began to wonder what that voice would sound like whispering sweet nothings to him in the bedroom. Damn it; he hadn't reacted like this since he first met Lydia.

"The Tower is bad news — it's that sudden catastrophic event that changes a life forever. It's the moment that shapes futures for good or ill. The Devil too, is not a good card. If it falls in a reading then I take it to mean that the querent is under the influence of wickedness in some form. But as we know, Inspector, wickedness can take many shapes, so the other cards in the spread would help with this."

She was silent for a moment. "The victim was male and elderly," she said at last. "So I'll offer this — the card has links to addiction, perhaps representing a man who benefits from the failings and addictions of those who fall under his spell."

Calladine kept his face inexpressive, but he was amazed. How could she know this? Albert North had been a notorious drug dealer on the Hobfield and many a poor soul had fallen foul of his particular brand of wickedness — but his identity and the nature of the death weren't generally known.

"You think your killer is matching cards to victims — isn't that so?" she asked.

"It's too early in the investigation to say. And the Tower?"

"The querent is about to experience, or has suffered, a huge change in their life: the metaphoric 'car crash' that happens out of the blue and leaves everything in ruins."

In Tariq Ahmed's case that was certainly true, but perhaps it was true of the killer too. Perhaps it was he or she who'd suffered that car crash?

"So whoever left these would understand the meanings?"

She shrugged. "Perhaps. Those particular cards are well known and have obvious interpretations. The meanings can be got from any book on the Tarot or even online."

"Do you sell many packs of these?"

"No, not really. I sell the jewellery, the incense and candles but the Tarot and other items used for divination are not particularly popular. If my customers want to know what the Tarot can tell them then they book a reading with me."

"Are readings popular?"

"Yes, very. The healing and development sessions we offer are also very popular. That is what I make most of my living from, Inspector."

She smiled at him and reached for a pack of tarot cards from the counter. "You are sceptical, I can tell. But no matter, I shall try to educate you."

Amaris Dean handed the pack to Calladine.

"Shuffle them, Inspector, then hand me three cards — any three you like."

He felt weird, no, he felt nervous, like a kid who'd unexpectedly set eyes on a girl he fancied, and yet all she did was make fun of him. He glanced at Ruth, who was smirking. She knew damn well what was going on, and she was enjoying every second of his discomfort.

Calladine couldn't concentrate, but he managed to shuffle the cards and make a random selection. As he handed the three cards to her he wondered what she could possibly glean from them. He was all fingers and thumbs, and as he handed the pack back a single card fell to the floor. Amaris gave him another of her dazzling smiles and bent to pick it up.

"We'll look at this one later."

He watched, fascinated, as she placed the three cards face up on her counter, her long, elegant fingers skimming over the images, her expression enigmatic.

"You have an issue you do not want to face, Inspector. It's an issue that has a history but you've only become aware of it recently. It concerns a woman." She ran her fingertips over one card in particular. "This card is the Queen of Pentacles. She is dark-haired and older than you. She is very close to you but is nonetheless a stranger." She looked up, her eyes questioning. "She is wealthy, powerful, and she is the woman who keeps a great secret. She also feels the need to resolve what happened in the past, Inspector."

Was she waiting for him to say something? Calladine wondered. Well, he wasn't going to. He shuffled uncomfortably as she placed the cards back in the pack.

"Now — the card you dropped."

She flicked it over. Even a novice could understand this one, Calladine thought. It was the Lovers. He didn't like the way this was going; she was teasing him. Her head was tilted to one side, and those eyes were making fun of him.

"You are a passionate man, Inspector, but passions can ebb and you are about to embark on something new and exciting. That's all I can say."

# CHAPTER 6

"What do you think?" Ruth asked.

"Load of rubbish." Calladine replied.

"You can't mean that. The things she said . . ."

"Where the case is concerned, fine. The meanings of those cards can be got from a variety of sources and she knows her stuff."

"Well, I think you're wrong. She was spot on about you. How could she possibly know those things?"

"She's a good psychologist. I bet with a bit of practice anyone could do it. I'm a cop and cops have complicated private lives, anyone could tell you that. I'm bound to have some dark secret in my past. And it'll be part of her stock in trade to be expert at body language. One way or another I'll have given her stuff. She picks up on reactions, things we don't even notice, and I'm an open book me."

"I think you're wrong. I can't just dismiss what she told us out of hand because I can't explain how she'd know. Psychology and body language doesn't cut it, not with me,."

"I think we've been had. Just as well we weren't paying for the lady's services."

"You can be so damn irritating at times, Tom Calladine. She said some personal stuff, specific personal stuff. How can you just dismiss that?"

He turned to Ruth. "Quite easily. And I bet you had a hand in it. Did you set me up?" He couldn't believe that Ruth would do that, but he did feel out of his depth here. Common sense said a big fat no, but somewhere in a far-flung corner of his mind was a huge question mark. Amaris Dean was odd — nice odd, good odd — and she came across as eminently plausible.

"No, of course I didn't!" Ruth protested. "You've got some cheek! Do you imagine I've got the time to go gossiping about your private life to a complete stranger just to prove a point? From that day to this I've not discussed your little problem with anyone."

He'd really put his foot in it. She sat in the passenger seat of the car, her arms folded and her face flushed.

"Okay, I apologise," he said hastily. "So let's just agree to disagree for now."

"Not good enough."

"Okay," he allowed, "as far as I'm concerned, the jury is out."

"Where you're concerned she got it dead right. You chose the cards; nothing was set up."

"Don't mention this to anyone else."

"I could hardly do that even if I wanted to. It's our little secret, remember?" She rolled her eyes. "But it really does need sorting. This whole thing about Eve Walker has been festering away between us for weeks. We need to have that talk and quick. You need to get this dealt with, get it out in the open. Your mother's gone and so's your dad — so I don't see why it should be such a secret."

"I wonder if Eve Walker thinks like you do? She might have very good reasons for wanting to keep me out of her life. She hasn't exactly come looking for me, has she?"

"According to Amaris she does want you. She said that the Queen of Pentacles felt the need to resolve things. So she wants to meet up; simple."

"Wanting to put things right and actually doing something about it are very different things, Ruth. Eve Walker may not be in any position to accept me. I could go storming in and hit a brick wall."

"She isn't Eve Walker anymore, either. She married." Ruth hesitated for moment. "Do you want to know more?"

"No, not yet. Save it."

He needed to get on with the job in hand. He'd take time to look at his personal life when they'd cracked this one. They were chasing a murderer; someone they had no clue about and who might intend to kill again.

"We'd better get back to the nick. Amaris Dean may have given us some insight into the meaning behind those cards but we're no further forward with the case. With any luck the CCTV will have thrown up something."

\* \* \*

And indeed it had. Back in the office, Rocco was obviously very excited about something.

"We've got a break, sir," he announced proudly. "It's hazy, but take a look," he said handing the inspector a photo.

"A man sat in a car," noted a puzzled Calladine, handing the photo back. "No woman, then?"

"No, just this, but it could prove a very useful find. The car belongs to one Sandy Cole, he's a private investigator. The plates on his car gave him away, and he has an office on the High Street."

"What's he doing there?"

"Apparently, one of Doctor Ahmed's neighbours is having an affair and he's been employed by the husband to gather evidence. He was there most of the evening and on into the night, and he was taking photographs."

"Go and talk to him some more, Rocco. Find out what he saw. If he had his camera handy then he might have photos of our killer . . . Imogen, is there anything else on Doctor Ahmed?"

"Nothing concrete. I spoke to the receptionist who runs his clinic and she confirmed that he wasn't easy to get on with. She said he didn't talk much, didn't socialise. Patients were always ringing up because they didn't understand what they'd been told or prescribed. He had a short fuse and didn't do long conversations." She shrugged. "Sounds like a right so and so; glad he was never treating anyone related to me."

"In that case, get his current patient list. He's upset someone; perhaps one of them had nothing to lose and decided to make him pay."

"Where does Albert North fit into that scenario?" Ruth asked.

"Well, he doesn't."

"So it's not just Doctor Ahmed that needed teaching a lesson?"

"Is that what you think this is all about: retribution?"

Ruth shrugged. "It's something to look at. Perhaps it's a disgruntled patient with links to Albert North — someone from the Hobfield?"

Ruth might have something there. They needed to do a lot more digging.

"Doc Hoyle on the phone, sir," Joyce called, holding out the handset for him.

"What's up, Doc?"

"I've finished the autopsies on both Ahmed and North, Tom. North really wasn't in good health. He had a failing heart and COPD."

"Any sign of cancer?"

"No, but he did have whiskey in his stomach. He must have drunk it minutes before his death."

"Did Julian find a bottle in his clothing?"

"No, there was nothing. Julian's gone back to the scene for another look around. Did your lot do a thorough search?"

"That was their job." Calladine rubbed his forehead. "So what are you saying?"

"No bottle on him so it could be that he was given the whiskey by his killer. Don't know if it helps; that's for you to work out."

"Thanks."

"The wound in Ahmed's back was caused by a long thin blade. Long because it went in a considerable distance, cutting the aorta virtually in two, and thin because the entry wound and path is narrow."

"A long thin knife, you say — unlikely to be one from the kitchen, then?"

"I'll leave that one with you too, Tom."

"I'll talk to Julian — see if he's found anything. I'm scratching my head on this one, I don't mind admitting. I'll consider anything, no matter how insignificant it might seem."

Once the doctor had hung up, Calladine immediately rang Julian Batho's mobile.

"Inspector! What can I do for you?"

"Are you at the scene yet, Julian?"

"I am. I'm scrambling around the weeds and litter under the bench where North was found as we speak."

Somehow the image didn't fit. Calladine couldn't imagine the serious-minded scientist down on his knees getting dirt all over his trousers.

"What is it you hope to find, Julian?"

"Something that might have contained whiskey, Inspector." His voice sounded strained, as if he was uncomfortable. "Something rather like this!" There was a brief pause and his tone became a lot lighter. "Inspector, I've just found the cup part of a flask. You know, the kind with a screw top, which you put hot drinks in. It was buried in the long grass under the bench where North was. It must have dropped during the attack. And it stinks of whiskey," he added jubilantly.

"Well done, Julian." Calladine was impressed. "Good work. Will you get it looked at as soon as? There might be prints, DNA from the killer, anything in fact."

"I know my job, Inspector," Julian replied tersely. "There were no prints on the petrol can. It looked fairly new and being a cold night, it's probable that our killer wore gloves. I'm also analysing the wig hair for DNA. With that, and now the cup, then we're in with a chance."

\* \* \*

"Why give him whiskey?" Ruth asked, after Calladine had relayed the new information.

"I've no idea, Ruth. Julian might come up with something to help."

"Shepherd's pie suit you?" she asked, flicking through the photos from the CCTV camera near Doctor Ahmed's house. "Supper tonight. Remember? You're coming round for a chat."

"The pie sounds fine, but the chat . . ." He shook his head. "I'm still not sure. I don't want to stir things up and then regret it."

Ruth shook her head.

"I know you think I'm being a real pain about this and you'd prefer me to drop it. But any normal person would want to know about their past, about their real parents. That's what you should want — it's what you need, and only then will you be able to deal with it."

"It's not that simple."

"Seems simple enough to me."

"Do I bring Lydia?" He ignored her comment.

"Not if you want to talk." She shot him a look. "It won't go away you know. It'll eat away at the back of your mind and end up keeping you awake nights."

"What will?" Imogen looked up, they had been talking too loudly. "Got a problem, sir?"

"Yep, the one over there glaring at me," he replied, pointing at Ruth. "Imogen, contact DI Greco at Oldston nick and tell him what you've got on the two missing girls. I'm going home for a bit to think. Don't ring me unless it's urgent."

# CHAPTER 7

"He wouldn't talk to me. Not a word." Lydia Holden slammed her briefcase down on the table and folded her arms. "He wants to see you first, Tom. He's insisting, and he won't give me anything until I persuade you to visit."

"I've told you before, I'm not going to see that thug in prison, so sorry, I can't help," Calladine said. The man had tried to kill him, here in this very room, surely she could understand? "Besides it wouldn't do — I'm a cop, remember? When Fallon comes up for trial I'll have to give evidence — so no, I can't go visit him, not even for you."

"You won't go, you mean. You're just being difficult, Tom. I need this story, you know that. You know what it would mean for my career so I can't see why you'd refuse to help me."

Calladine sighed. He'd known it was bound to come to this. Lydia's obsession with his cousin had reached an all-time high. She was like a starving dog with a bone. God knows what she expected Fallon to tell her. He was hardly going to implicate himself in other crimes, was he? And that's what talking candidly to Lydia would mean.

"My advice is drop it — drop the story and certainly drop Fallon. You shouldn't go back. You'll be called to give evidence too, you know. It was you that brought him here that day."

"I did not!" she protested. "Well, not willingly." She sniffed. "He hijacked me and my car. You know that, so how can you imply that I was somehow on his side?"

"Because you deliberately went out to find him. You spoke to his wife that day. You stopped her on the street and spun her some yarn about dogs to win her trust. Just like Marilyn that; she was always far too gullible. Fallon will have a crack defence team working for him. He won't go down without a fight, so that and your cosy little visits to Strangeways will be something they'll use."

Those full pink lips pouted at him in that way that usually made him cave in. He groaned inwardly. He hated arguing with her but this was something he wouldn't compromise on.

"You're being much too stubborn. I don't think you want me to be a success, do you? You want me to go back to being a provincial hack so I can be at your beck and call forever more. Well, that's not going to happen," she assured him, her hands on her hips. "So get used to it. I've had enough. And while we're at it, what are you doing all dressed up? Where are you going?"

"I'm not dressed up. I've just got my blue suit on, that's all." He was trying to decide between two ties, one a gift from Lydia, the other one his mother had given him. "Ruth's asked me round for something to eat."

"And I am not invited?"

"No, it's a work thing," he lied.

"Well, in that case I'm going up to bed and I don't want company!" With that she flounced off in the direction of the staircase.

With Lydia a sulk could last for some time.

"You're not even going to try to put things right, are you, Tom Calladine?" she shouted down to him. "You're an idiot you've let me down!"

"I said I'd be there at seven," he said, doing his best to ignore her diatribe. "I can't disappoint her." He heard the bedroom door slam shut, winced, and decided to put on the tie which his mother had given him.

\* \* \*

"You're a difficult man to pin down," Rocco told the man, who sat at a huge desk in a dimly lit office on Leesdon High Street. "I've been hanging around for over an hour waiting for you to show."

"That's the nature of the business, I'm afraid. I seem to spend most of my time parked up somewhere in my car, camera lens pressed against a window. But you can always get me on my mobile." He smiled at Rocco and handed him a business card.

Rocco pulled his warrant card from his pocket. "DC Simon Rockliffe, Leesdon CID."

The man stood up and proffered his hand. "Pleased to meet you. I'm Sandy Cole, private investigator," he said proudly.

He was a heavily built man with red hair. He had a florid face and a small moustache; and was wearing a tweed jacket, a check shirt and a bow tie. Rocco wondered why he'd never noticed him around Leesdon before.

"We spoke briefly on the phone earlier about the murder in Hopecross," Rocco said, seating himself on the chair facing Sandy Cole. "You were there last night, keeping watch on a house down the road. Given the timescale we're looking at, you must have seen the killer pass by. We're probably looking for a woman. We don't know her age but she was possibly dressed as an elderly woman. She'd have been going to a house three doors up from the one you were watching."

Rocco gave Sandy Cole a few moments to think about it then watched as he accessed a file of photos on his computer.

"This could be her. I snapped her almost unconsciously — I was taking photos of anything that moved — out of boredom." He laughed. "People think I live such a glamorous life but they're quite wrong — it's sheer hard slog that wins a case in the end."

"Same with us, mate."

"But I do remember her, mainly because of the way she was walking. She had a stick and was sort of hunched, as if she was in pain. She was talking to herself as well. I couldn't hear what she was saying of course, I was too far away."

"Did she have anything with her?"

"A bag, quite small and tucked under her arm," Sandy said, examining his images. "And the stick; she was leaning on it quite heavily."

"Was the bag big enough to hold a weapon, a large knife for example?"

"No, it was more like one of those little clutch jobs. Here she is." He beckoned Rocco to his side of the desk. "Knifed then, was she?"

"I'm not supposed to say. Not yet anyway."

The image wasn't particularly clear but Sandy was able to enlarge and enhance it somewhat as Rocco looked. It was definitely a woman. Her face was fuzzy in the poor light but she had the right colour hair — grey — and was wearing glasses.

"It could be the stick, you know." Sandy zoomed in closer. "See, it's one of those old jobbies. They sometimes had a blade hidden inside. That could be your murder weapon. I'll print you a copy and email the original. She was going three doors up as you say. I've got a good one of his other visitor, and unlike this one, she was a regular. I've been staking out that road for over a week now and she's there most nights."

Another visitor? The team were under the impression that the good doctor didn't have much of a social life.

"Who is it, do you know? Rocco asked.

"No, but she's a looker," Sandy said, showing him a second photo. "See what I mean? Quite a stunner. She very often stays all night — something going on there, mark my words."

So Tariq Ahmed hadn't been the loner after all — he'd obviously had a lady friend. But who was she and more to the point why hadn't she come forward?

* * *

"She let you out, then?" Ruth greeted him at her front door. "Come in!"

"I do as I please. Lydia doesn't run my life you know," Calladine replied, annoyed at her remark. "She'd like to but I can be quite firm when pushed."

"Glad to hear it. What's she working on currently?"

"My bloody cousin — as ever. In fact we've just had words about it. We don't often argue, but just lately she's become hard work. Lydia says he won't talk to her. My gut tells me he's up to something, but I can't think what. I've a shrewd idea he's using her to get to me again. I've no idea what he'd want but I intend to stay well away. I've brought a bottle of red." He proffered the bottle he had tucked under his arm. "It's a good one."

"So I see." She smiled as she led the way into the sitting room.

"Hi Tom!" Jake Ireson greeted him. "I'm going to leave you two to it. I've got a mountain of marking to get through — mock A levels." He grimaced.

Tom saw the pile of papers and books and didn't envy him his job.

"He's already eaten," Ruth told Tom. "So there's no excuse; we can have that talk now."

"What talk?" Jake asked.

"You keep out of it," Ruth warned lightly. "Tom and I have some old business — family business — that needs sorting."

"See you later, then," Jake said, giving them both a smile.

"Are you two getting on better these days?"

"We're getting on very well, Tom. He's really good to have around, and I've decided that I wouldn't want to be without him."

Calladine wasn't in the mood to hear any romantic stuff, not while things between him and Lydia were so strained. But he was pleased Ruth had found someone, of course he was. She deserved to be happy. But then so did he. All he seemed to do was go round in circles. First there'd been Monika, steady and always there, until Lydia had crashed into his life. Lydia was utterly different from Monika and his attraction to her had been instant. But now — he didn't know how he felt. Lydia was demanding and he couldn't deliver, not while he was working. Things were only going to get worse.

"You've got the place nice." Calladine changed the subject. "You've decorated — and you've bought some new furniture."

"We chose the stuff together. We wanted to make the place *ours* and not just mine. We decided it made sense for Jake to move in with me," she explained. "His old place was a flat, and he has the dog. I have a nice big garden here."

"Where is the dog?"

"He's had to have a small op, so he's staying at the veterinary hospital tonight."

"Expensive!"

"Insurance — we're not that daft." She laughed.

"So — you and Jake . . . it's looking serious, then."

Ruth smiled. If he had to put a word to the way she looked right now it would have been *enigmatic*. "Well? Are you two an item, a proper item, or what?"

She laughed again and he watched her take a single glass from the cupboard. Not important, but why wasn't she joining him?

"I certainly hope so," she replied, and then paused for a few seconds. "I really don't want to do the next bit on my own." A small smile hovered about her lips.

She was trying to tell him something. He scratched his head. He hated it when women got like this. There was an odd sort of silence. He could hear the antique clock ticking, and she still had that weird smile on her face.

"I'm pregnant, Tom," she said at last, averting her gaze from his.

There was another, longer silence. Had he heard her right? Had Ruth Bayliss really just told him that she was with child? He banged his right ear lightly — perhaps he was hearing things.

"Pregnant," he repeated, as if he'd no idea what the word meant.

"But don't you dare tell anyone. It's still early days." She handed him the glass and went to find a corkscrew.

Tom Calladine watched her walk back into the kitchen. This was a bombshell. She was pregnant. His sergeant. The woman who'd been his work partner for so long that he couldn't recall when she hadn't been around, was going to have a child! How come he hadn't guessed?

"How did that happen?" he asked, following her and feeling foolish for asking. "I mean — is it what you want? A child? At your age?"

Her eyes widened and she gave him a little slap with the back of her hand. It was okay — the awkwardness between them had evaporated as quickly as it had appeared.

"Don't be so rude! Women today, they have kids at all ages. And we're thrilled, both of us. Me and Jake — we couldn't be happier."

"What will you do about work? What about us?" he asked, suddenly horrified at the prospect of losing her to domesticity and motherhood. "I don't think I could work with anyone else," he admitted.

He could have bitten his tongue off. That sounded so selfish. She had every right to be thrilled, and he, silly bugger, was only thinking about work.

\* \* \*

But that was the crux of it. Ruth knew how well they worked together and how long that relationship had taken to hone.

She laughed off his remark, but she was secretly flattered that he could acknowledge that he needed her. They were a solid team that had been built up over years of solving cases together and trusting each other's judgement. She reckoned he was one of the best. She admired him; his intelligence and insight, the way he operated. As far as she was concerned no one else came close.

"Tom Calladine where's your professionalism?" she teased. "Having a baby won't finish me, idiot. I'll be back. I'll take a few months off then I'll be back as normal. You'll have to make do with Rocco for a bit, that's all."

"That is supposed to reassure me, is it? Motherhood, babies, they can do strange things to a woman's reasoning powers. Your powers of detection could be irreparably impaired — not to mention what this revelation's doing to my head."

"Get over yourself, that's old-fashioned sexist thinking. A few months and I'll be back. With a bit of luck you won't even realise I've been gone."

"I'm pleased for you both, of course I am, but are you sure you'll cope?"

"No, I'm not, but I won't do any worse than every other mother," was her curt reply. "Come on, smile. You look as if you've just got the worst news ever. You must have realised it was bound to happen sooner or later."

"I didn't really think about it," he admitted. "I'll miss you though. Rocco isn't the same. He's good, but not the same."

"You'll be fine. Rocco and Imogen, they'll both look after you. Shall we eat, and forget the baby news for now? We've got you to sort out, remember? That's why you're here tonight."

"Not sure I'm ready — if I'll ever be ready. And anyway, do we have to spoil the evening, and your great news, with this?"

"We're not spoiling the evening," Ruth insisted, depositing the tin box on the dining table. "It's time you took ownership of this. You need to look at the letters and photos inside. Really look."

"You said you were making pie?"

"Pour yourself some wine and I'll get it."

She disappeared into the kitchen and returned with a steaming hot dish of shepherd's pie. She gestured for him to sit and proceeded to serve.

"You're a good cook."

"I know, and you have eaten here before. You know I like to cook if I have the time. There's some red cabbage there if you want some."

"Pie and red cabbage. Reminds me of school dinners." He grinned.

"This is nothing like a school dinner, don't be so damned cheeky!"

\* \* \*

Fifteen minutes later the pie dish was empty. Ruth smiled. Calladine was like Jake: he had a good appetite. She watched him help himself to more wine. He tapped on the lid of the box.

"It's the fact that she never told me."

He frowned. "Not even a hint in all those years. She never said a bad word about my dad either, well, nothing above and beyond the normal spats all married couples have."

"She obviously didn't hold it against him. She accepted you and what had happened, and got on with things."

"She must have been angry though, when she found out. He had another woman, for God's sake, and not only that, he'd got her pregnant. Mum couldn't have children; she said so in the letter, so she must have been jealous. My dad's mistress has his child then expects my mum to bring me up."

"Things were different then. People's behaviour was different. Unmarried mothers were frowned upon, and Freda loved you, remember. You were the innocent party, an infant, probably quite cute too." Ruth grinned.

"Probably very cute in fact." He smiled back. "I still think this is a bad idea. I should leave things alone. I should take this tin box and stash it in my attic, out of sight."

"That won't make it go away, Tom. The issues will still be there."

"What issues? I'm not going to make an issue of anything."

He was at it again — refusing to face up to things. He was one of the most level-headed men she knew, so why was his personal life always such a mess? Ruth was about to lay into him when Calladine's mobile rang. It was Rocco.

* * *

"I've got something, sir!" he began excitedly. "Doctor Ahmed had a lady friend. She went to his house the night he was killed. I got a photo of her from Sandy Cole and Joyce recognised her straight away, so we know who she is. "

"Have you spoken to her?"

"No, sir. She's on duty at the hospital. I was going to go and speak to her but I thought I'd better tell you first. It's his registrar, Samantha Hurst. Hurst is her married name, sir. Prior to that she was Samantha Buckley, you know one of *the* Buckleys."

The Buckley family was like royalty in Leesworth. Calladine knew they owned a large factory on Leesworth Industrial Estate, and employed numbers of the local population. The woman would have to be interviewed and she might even become a suspect, but for now, they'd tread carefully.

"In that case we'll go see her together in the morning, Rocco. You've been at it all day, so go home and have a rest. Good work. You've done well."

A breakthrough of sorts at last, something they really needed. He took another swig of the wine.

"What's Rocco got?" Ruth asked.

"Turns out our unsociable doctor had a woman in his life. A woman nobody told us about, not even Ms Celia Downs, and I can't believe she didn't know."

"Why, who is she?"

"His registrar, Doctor Samantha Hurst — the former Samantha Buckley no less."

At the sound of the name he saw Ruth's face fall then turn several shades paler than normal.

"One of the pharmaceutical Buckleys?"

"I believe so, yes," he confirmed.

"In that case we might have a problem."

# CHAPTER 8

"Why? We'll go easy and do our best not to upset anybody."

"No, it's not that." Ruth cleared her throat. "This is one time in my life when I really wish I could have a glass of wine."

She had him worried now — what was it she knew?

"You need to know about Eve Walker," she told him finally.

"No, I don't. I've told you what I'm going to do."

"No, you don't understand. You must listen to me. You can't go haring off tomorrow without knowing the truth."

"You're persistent if nothing else. What truth? This?" He rapped on the box. "This is my personal life. It won't interfere with my work. I won't let it."

"This time it might." She paused, looking up at his puzzled face. "You see, she's not Walker anymore. She got married years ago."

"Ruth, please. I can live without this and especially now." She was making him edgy. He was nowhere near ready for the truth about his past, so why couldn't she leave it like he'd asked?

"No, you can't live without it for one very good reason."

There was a silence. Ruth was staring at him. He couldn't make her out. What was it she knew, and why all the going on about that bloody tin?

"You have to know because she's Eve Buckley now."

More silence as the penny dropped.

"Buckley — as in . . ?"

"Yes, Tom, as in the pharmaceutical Buckleys," she confirmed. "So you see, you do need to know because this Samantha, the woman you're going to interview in the morning, is your half-sister."

He was stunned. A half-sister — a sibling. Another bit of knowledge that terrified him. How was it that he kept discovering female family members he never knew he had? First his daughter Zoe had turned up out of the blue, now suddenly he had a sister.

"I'm sorry, Tom, but you can see why I couldn't just leave it. You might not want to know them, but Eve Buckley will know all about you."

Ruth was right; she would probably know, and that could well put him at a disadvantage. What if Samantha was involved in the murders? Now that would really cause him a problem. He scowled. Why now? Why all this when he wasn't up to dealing with it? His stomach churned. He was trying to think. What did he know about that family? There was another one — he'd seen his name in the local paper — 'entrepreneur of the year' or something. The son, Simon Buckley, had run the factory since the death of his father. So he had a half-brother as well. It was making his head hurt. He wasn't ready to sort this out.

"I'm sorry Ruth but this is too much to take in. I think I'll just go home. I need some time alone to work all this out. My head's spinning."

"You can't drive; you've drunk most of that wine and you're tipsy. Jake will take you. He needs to get petrol for tomorrow anyway," she said, getting up to go and fetch him.

It had been a night and a half and he couldn't take any more. Fresh air was what he needed, that and a gallon of coffee. He hoped Lydia had calmed down. He didn't relish the idea of arguing afresh about Fallon, not now, not with all this on his mind. Perhaps he should just tell her and get it all out in the open.

"Take it with you," Ruth said pushing the tin box into his hand. "It can't do you any more harm. You know its secrets now."

"More's the pity," he said, kissing her cheek. "Thanks. Lovely meal. I'll be better company in the morning, once I've mulled it over. No need to drag Jake out, I'll leave my car here and walk. It's hardly miles, is it? Just along the High Street."

"You'll be alright?"

"Course — what d'you imagine I'm going to do? I'm not a child, you know. I just want to clear my head. Sort all this out," he said, shaking the box.

He turned his overcoat collar up against the biting wind, tucked the box under his arm and stuffed his hands in his pockets.

One meal, an evening spent with a friend, and he had a whole heap of stuff to think about. Ruth pregnant — he never thought he'd see the day. He smiled. It was good, it really was — she'd make a great mum and Jake would be great too. They were good together. Pity he couldn't find that special someone like Ruth had. Lydia wasn't settling down material; she was far too ambitious. She wanted fun and excitement. For her, he was merely a means to an end, a channel for the information she needed. It was a sobering thought. And then there was the Buckley thing. The Buckley thing made him feel sick.

It was only Wednesday night but the High Street was busy. A group of men were noisily drawing attention to themselves outside the Wheatsheaf pub. Someone shouted, and he heard a bottle smash. It wasn't that late but it was already shaping up to be a wild one.

Calladine turned down a side street. He'd go down the back lane and reach his home that way. He wasn't in any mood to run the gauntlet of the other pubs strung along Leesdon's main thoroughfare.

"Detective Inspector!" The voice sounded from in front of him.

He'd got his head down against the wind so he hadn't noticed the pool of light coming from the shop window. Amaris Dean was sweeping up the rubbish from the footpath outside her shop.

He looked up. She was smiling, and for a moment he was speechless. Her long hair flowed in soft waves down her back and was held away from her face with a wide band. Her skirt seemed to flow as well, right down to her ankles. There was something of the gipsy about her and he liked it.

"You're open late," he noted, feeling the butterflies start.

She smiled. "We've had a development session here tonight."

He'd no idea what she meant but he nodded and smiled back anyway. For a woman who must be close to his own age, she was in good nick. She wasn't wearing much makeup, just a little lipstick and something that seemed to make her eyes look all smoky and sexy.

"You keep long hours — a bit like me." He couldn't think of anything else to say. He was as tongue-tied as an inept teenager talking to a girl he fancied for the first time. "You still have to travel home, then?"

"No, I live up there," she said pointing to the first floor. "I have a lovely flat above my shop. Fancy a drink, Tom?" She smiled again.

She had that look in her eyes, the one that made him feel sure she could see into his very soul.

"You don't mind if I call you Tom, do you?"

She was still gazing at him, her eyes holding him. No he certainly didn't; she could call him anything she wanted. He was attracted to her, but it wasn't just that. There was something else too, which for now he'd put down to fascination.

"You look . . . troubled," she said, tilting her head to one side. "You almost walked right past. Work, is it? Case getting you down?"

"Something like that," he replied following her into the shop.

"You should learn how to relax. Perhaps I could show you some techniques."

"Like what?"

"Relaxation. You could even come here and try a reiki session."

Something else he didn't understand.

"What did you mean — development session? What is it that's being developed?"

She laughed and picked up a bottle from the table. It was a vodka bottle but the fluid inside was pink. He was staring again — was nothing about this woman ordinary?

"My special cranberry vodka," she told him. "Here, try some. It's lovely at this time of year, warming and festive." Her eyes twinkled as she handed him a generous glassful.

Calladine sipped the pink liquid cautiously, but she was right, it was delicious.

"Some of my customers show potential, for example in healing or mediumship," she explained. "I hold workshops, invite a guest speaker and we go from there."

"You've been busy, then?"

"Oh yes, Tom, that's what it's all about. Every session I hold here helps to generate business for my shop. But by far the most popular are the tarot readings."

Still clutching the vodka, he followed her upstairs to her flat. The sitting room was a delight — a cosy oasis far from the busy high street. She had the place decorated in subtle tones of pale green with bead curtains between the rooms. There were two large squashy sofas festooned with colourful cushions either side of an Edwardian fireplace. The place was warm, relaxing. She also had a number of paintings on her walls, some looked a little esoteric and there was a fabulous nude. His gaze fell on it and he couldn't tear his eyes away. The woman was posing on a fur mat and her hair fell long and lustrous down her back. But it was her eyes, that steady regard, that finally made him turn and look at her quizzically.

"Yes," she nodded, a smile hovering on those full lips. "That is me — a good few years ago now though."

She was a truly gorgeous woman, and the painting simply confirmed it. Calladine sat on the sofa, sinking into the plump cushions. He checked his mobile — nothing, no messages and no missed calls. He turned the thing off, which was unusual for him but it wouldn't hurt for once. The vodka warmed him and somewhere in the background soft music was playing. He yawned, and the day's problems slipped away as he closed his eyes.

\* \* \*

*Thursday*

"Where the hell have you been? You've been gone all night, no word, no text, nothing!" A furious Lydia greeted him the next morning.

She was standing in his kitchen, dressed for work in a crisp suit, her hands on her hips as she glared at him. Her blonde hair was loose and fell over her shoulders. She looked glorious. Why did he feel so guilty? He'd done nothing wrong.

"I told you, I went to Ruth's . . . we had a lot to discuss," he explained with a shrug, as if it was no big deal. But, of course he knew very well it was. It was a very big deal in fact because Amaris Dean had got to him. Which would explain why he felt like a naughty teenager.

"You left about ten. I rang her. And you turned your mobile off — you never turn your mobile off, Tom. So what's going on?" she demanded angrily. "I'll ask once again, where have you been all night?"

"I fell asleep," he replied lamely. It was true, after all. He'd drunk the vodka and fallen asleep on Amaris's sofa. But he could hardly tell Lydia that — she had no idea about Amaris. Anyway, it wasn't as if Amaris was a rival or anything. Who was he kidding?

"It's not good enough, Tom. None of it is, and I can't go on like this anymore."

Alarm bells were going off inside his head.

"You don't come home, you don't want to help with my work, our relationship is crashing and you don't give a damn, do you?"

"Of course I do." He was struggling. "I had a lot of thinking to do, things I discussed with Ruth." Not a lie — what about the Eve Buckley problem?

"You're always talking to Ruth. Don't you ever consider talking things over with me for a change?"

"I don't want to burden you. Apart from you, she's one of the few people I can talk to."

"You never tell me anything and you don't take me anywhere any more. You've become a huge bore, Tom Calladine, and it's not good enough, not by a long way." She turned on her heel and marched off into the kitchen.

What had he done? Well, she wasn't going to believe any explanation he gave her. Perhaps he should take her out more and make a fuss of her, but the truth was, at the end of a hard day he just didn't have the energy. It was the age gap beginning to show, as he had known it inevitably would. For now Calladine just needed to shower and change and get off to work. Lydia was fast becoming an irritation he could do without.

"It's six thirty, and I'm off soon. You'd better drink this." She handed him a mug of hot coffee.

He took the drink gratefully and downed it. He had to get his head together. Today was a big day. He rubbed his face and yawned.

"Off where? Not back to the prison, surely? You're not going back to see that villain? He's playing you; you shouldn't go near him."

"I'll do what I like, Detective," she said with her nose in the air. "But I'm not going to see Fallon today; I'm going to find myself an apartment to rent."

He looked at her. She stood clutching a suitcase in each hand. "Just like that?"

"No, not just like that. We've both seen this coming. You've got your work now, and you've fallen back into your old habits. Work, booze, sleep, that's your life, Tom. You don't have room for romance, and you certainly don't have room for me."

"That's not true — we're good together. You looked after me while I was ill. I thought we had something, were going somewhere . . ."

"Going where, exactly, Detective? Because I'm not for settling down, not for a long while. And when I do decide to, my life will be a lot different from the one you seem to be offering."

"My job's very demanding," he mumbled.

"So's mine, and they're not compatible."

"Where will you go?"

"Like I said, I'm looking for a flat, but in the meantime Zoe and Jo have said I can have their spare room."

That was a good one — his own daughter taking in his estranged lover!

## CHAPTER 9

"It's barely seven in the morning! Why so early? Can't it wait, Harriet?" Gordon Lessing asked, annoyed. "I've got work. My haulage business won't run itself you know. This is most inconvenient."

*More inconvenient than he realises*, the voice purred in Harriet's head.

"You know how ill I am, and this won't wait. I still have things that belonged to Sybil. You should have them — jewellery and other items she gave me."

He didn't reply but she could almost hear the gears turning. He would want Sybil's stuff if he thought it might be valuable. He was a greedy sod, so the thought of getting something for nothing, something he could sell on, was the hook she needed.

"You know how I'm fixed, Gordon. I'm trying to leave things straight." She cleared her throat. "It's all good quality; most of it belonged to our mother. Your Jane gave it to me after Sybil died. But it should go back to her now — I've no use for it. There're some family papers too. Jane is into all that genealogy stuff so she'll appreciate it."

Jane was Gordon and Sybil's only child — now the last of the line.

"Do you want me to come and collect it?"

"No I'll bring it round in the car later. You said you had some props we could borrow for the show at the church hall, remember? The magician's paraphernalia. I thought I could take a look while I'm at it. You've no idea how difficult it is to get that sort of stuff. I know I'm not well, but I did promise the committee that I'd ask you."

Harriet was part of a team who organised regular shows and the annual pantomime at the village hall. She didn't appear — she was far too shy, but she was happy to sew costumes and find props where she could. This year the show was to be a revue. There was a surprising amount of talent in Leesdon, including a young man who had aspirations to be a magician. But he had no stage props.

"Yes, I suppose that's alright. I'm here this morning until about ten, but then I have to go out."

"Thank you, Gordon. I'll be round within the hour."

Harriet knew that her brother-in-law had been an avid collector of theatrical bits and pieces for years, the older and the more unusual the better. He kept it all in his cellar — exactly where she wanted him to be.

*He'll take you down there but he won't come back,* the voice reminded her in a gleeful tone.

Harriet was excited. Gordon Lessing was the big one. She'd get him to take her down into that dark, damp cellar of his and there he'd breathe his last: cold, battered and in agony.

*Serves him right — d'you think Sybil wasn't cold when he did what he did to her?*

The voice was right. Sybil had been trapped for days in the dead of winter with a head injury and a broken femur, and with no way of calling for help. Lessing had done that. When she was found her poor sister was very close to death from hypothermia. She'd also lost a lot of blood, and had stood little chance of survival despite the hospital's best efforts. The medics dismissed what she'd told them as delirium. But Harriet knew differently.

Sybil had told her weeks before that Lessing wanted her dead and that she was scared. At the time Harriet had dismissed this as pure fantasy. Sybil took medication for depression. She got obsessed about things. Harriet had put her sister's fears down to the side effects.

But Sybil had kept on; she wouldn't let it drop no matter how much reassurance Harriet gave her. Then one day when Gordon had had too much to drink and was lying comatose on the sofa, Sybil has shown her the stuff on his phone. There were messages, and video footage of the girls, but most frightening of all was the photo of Yuri, his contact.

It was then that Harriet had realised that her sister was right and Gordon Lessing was capable of anything. It was obvious from the contents of the phone that he was part of a people trafficking ring specialising in the kidnapping of young children. But what to do about it? She'd told Sybil to be on her guard, and to give him no reason to suspect that she knew.

But poor Sybil must have let something slip. Lessing was a clever man. He'd got away with his involvement in this evil trade for years, so dealing with a frail, sickly woman gave him no problems.

It wasn't until after her sister's death that Harriet pieced it together. She knew he'd driven them both to their caravan by the coast. They'd stayed for the weekend and then he'd said he had to return home alone because of work and that Sybil had wanted to stay on. But Harriet couldn't understand that. Sybil hated being alone and, it being winter, the park would be deserted.

Given her injuries, he must have hit her with a heavy object. He had taken a wrench or something similar to her head and leg, and left her for dead. He'd been clever too, setting things up so it looked like a robbery gone wrong. He'd told the police that when she didn't ring he'd become worried and had gone to find out what had happened. No one could find any evidence that Sybil's death had anything to do with him. Harriet vowed at poor Sybil's funeral that she would make him pay. She was going to make him talk too — about everything. He'd confess to killing Sybil and he'd confess to the kidnap of the children. Harriet shuddered. She'd beat a confession out of him if she had to, and record it for the police.

* * *

"You look awful," Ruth said, raising her head from the pile of papers on her desk. "The result of going walkabout last night, I presume. Want to tell me about it?"

"Can't look that bad." He rubbed his chin.

"Well, you do," she hissed. "And I don't know what you think you're doing, but Lydia was on the phone half the night. I hardly got a wink of sleep. I was worried about you too, idiot! Why didn't you just ring her and let her know where you were?"

"Because I fell asleep."

"You are kidding? I mean where could you possibly put your head down between mine and yours?"

"I bumped into someone, a friend, we had a drink, and well . . ."

"Well what? What are you talking about, and what friend?"

He'd have to tell her. She'd go on and on until she wheedled the truth out of him anyway, so why not just get it over with?

"Amaris Dean." He cleared his throat.

"I see."

No, she didn't. She had that expression on her face, the unimpressed one, as she shook her head. As far as Ruth was concerned, he was at it again. Now he'd have to explain, in detail, because she'd want to know the lot.

"You never learn, do you? After the debacle with Monika I thought you'd do things differently but no, you carry on making the same old mistakes. You've still got Lydia at home. Remember her? The woman you're supposed to be nuts about? The one you don't deserve."

79

"You've changed your tune," he replied.

"But still you go chasing after some other poor unsuspecting female without clearing up the problem of the old one first. She'll find out, you know. Lydia is a smart cookie and when she does I wouldn't want to be in the firing line."

"Amaris isn't poor, and I doubt she's unsuspecting. In fact I think she's great. She makes great vodka too."

"If she's distilling her own alcohol — that's illegal."

"No, she steeps cranberries in it, makes a lovely mix, very moreish."

"So you got drunk, and slept where — in her bed?"

"Don't be daft, I hardly know the woman. No, I dossed down on her sofa. Unintentional I should add. But when I woke up she'd taken off my shoes, plumped a couple of pillows around my head and covered me in a duvet. Lovely woman, lots of promise. I reckon she quite likes me."

"Then she wants her head looking at — and you too. Lydia will skin you alive when she finds out."

"I don't think Lydia cares anymore . . . Actually, she's left me."

He winced. Ruth was looking at him long and hard.

"How come you are able to deliver news like that with nothing more than a cursory shrug? Not so long ago Lydia Holden meant the world to you."

"Things change, people change; you know that."

"And there was me thinking you might actually make a go of it with the woman. Well, I can't say I blame her. Finally seen you for what you are, has she? Does she know about Amaris already? You weren't stupid enough to tell her, have you?"

"No, and don't you go telling her either. She's fed up, that's all. She's had enough of me not being much fun, that and my reluctance to get involved with Fallon again has ruined it."

Calladine was well aware that Ruth knew all about his hatred of his cousin and Lydia's desire for him to get in contact with Fallon. But did Ruth understand that Lydia's reasons were purely selfish? Lydia still believed that Fallon could somehow benefit her career.

"So where's she gone?"

"She's staying with Zoe and Jo for the time being. Can you believe that? My own daughter is putting her up! She'll be expecting me to make some grand gesture so that she can come back . . . Trouble is I don't know if that's what I want. I'm all out of grand gestures where Lydia's concerned. I know it sounds mad, given how things have been the last few months, but now that she's gone I feel sort of relieved."

"Because now you can chase after Amaris Dean with a clear conscience. That's what you mean, isn't it? You are an idiot, Tom Calladine. Don't you ever want to settle down?"

"Lydia was never the settling down type. You warned me often enough."

"Lydia's good for you. I know she can be single-minded and likes to get her own way but my advice is, make that grand gesture: forget all about Amaris Dean. Can you do that?"

Instead of replying he wandered over to the incident board. It was a good job they were alone in here. He wouldn't want the others hearing any of this.

"You told anyone your news yet?"

"No, and don't you, either. It's too soon; we will tell folk after the first scan."

"You told me."

"You're not folk, are you?" She gave him another stern look. "You're practically family; and I trust you to keep it shut. And it's because I care about you that I'm telling you to put things straight with Lydia. Get Amaris Dean out of your head because she'll only give you trouble."

Ruth's advice was too late. Amaris Dean was already giving him trouble. She was in his head and he couldn't stop thinking about her. But he didn't want to discuss it any more.

"Who's going to see Samantha Hurst?" he asked.

"I thought you and me would go. She's got a clinic until eleven and then she's free."

"I can't go, can I?"

"Why not? You've got to meet her sometime."

"I can't go because she's a relative, and she could end up a suspect in a murder case. You'll have to take Rocco with you."

"She's not likely to be involved, not really, is she?"

At that moment both Imogen and Rocco entered the incident room, so they took the conversation into Calladine's office.

"Rocco will wonder what's going on. Interviewing Samantha Hurst is too important for him not to," she said, closing the door.

"Never mind all that and for heaven's sake don't tell him anything. Just ascertain the nature of the relationship between her and Ahmed. It looks like she's the only person who knew Doctor Ahmed well enough to give us any information. She can probably determine if anything is missing from his house. Take her there, walk her around and see what she says."

"And you? What are your plans for the morning?"

"I'd thought I go see Doc Hoyle and check what forensics has turned up. I should tell Julian about Samantha. Ask if she'll volunteer a DNA sample and fingerprints when you see her."

"Okay then, I'll take Rocco, but the minute she ceases to be of interest to the case you face up to things."

His face was grey again, his mouth pulled into a thin line. He knew Ruth was right but he couldn't face meeting his newly discovered family, not yet. And if he saw anyone first then it would have to be Eve Buckley herself.

* * *

Two mugs of coffee and a quick look at the Cassidy/Prideau files provided more questions than answers. What were Thorpe and his lot doing about the missing girl? She was only four years old for God's sake, and she'd been gone for nearly a week. Imogen's research had thrown up a very real possibility, too, so why weren't those goons on the other team taking any notice?

"Imogen, have you spoken to Oldston nick about this?" Calladine asked, placing the file back on her desk. "Because I think you should. Your research and theories have merit, and that lead you got can't just be ignored."

"You mean the mutual friends thing on the social media site?"

"Yep, exactly that."

"I did give the DI dealing with the Leah Cassidy case a ring but he was out and he hasn't got back to me."

"Well, ring him again and keep on ringing until you get somewhere. The two missing girls are linked. Whoever took Leah Cassidy also took Isla Prideau, I'll bet on it. This needs sorting before some other poor kid goes missing."

Apart from him, Imogen and Joyce, the room was empty. Ruth and Rocco had gone. He should feel relieved but he didn't; he just felt as though he'd let Ruth down. He knew he'd have to face up to this sooner or later. He stuck his hands in his trouser pockets and gazed at the incident board.

What was it telling him — the faces, the methods, and then the mystery of those strange cards? What was it Amaris had suggested — that the killer was matching cards to victims? And was that really their killer — that blurry image of an elderly woman walking along the avenue Ahmed had lived on? It seemed unlikely. But if they could find her, perhaps she could give them something. She could have seen someone, a car, heard shouting, anything.

He coughed and moved a little closer. A thought occurred to him, took form and became a distinct possibility in his mind. Why hadn't he seen it before? But it was obvious now that he'd realised.

The old feeling was back — that feeling he got when he spotted something significant. The murderer wasn't just matching the cards to the victims — it was also the way they were killed. That was the link. The way each victim died was somehow meaningful to the bastard. So it was about revenge after all.

"Joyce, could you do something? Look back in the records and see if there is anything that links Albert North to a fatality involving fire."

# CHAPTER 10

"Heavy night?" was the doctor's greeting. "You look as if you should consider doing something else too."

"What do you mean, 'too'?" Calladine asked as the doctor pushed a pamphlet at him.

"Retirement made easy," the doc smiled knowingly, "for folk like you and me — of a certain age and wedded to the job."

"I'm not ready for all that bollocks just yet," was the inspector's scathingly reply. "I lay on that sofa of mine for weeks on end, and it was no way to live, I'm telling you."

"You must have hobbies, Tom, something you like to do in your free time?"

"No — that's just it, Doc, I'm a cop. I get up a cop and go to bed a cop. My head's permanently full of cop stuff, so no, I don't do hobbies. I leave that up to Ruth." He smiled. "Do you know she spent her last spot of leave watching some bloody birds in the centre of Manchester?"

"That'd be the peregrines," he replied knowingly. "Success story, that one, Tom."

"Whatever it is, it's not for me."

Doc Hoyle sighed heavily. "That's what I suspected. This isn't the answer for either of us, is it?" He tossed the pamphlet into the bin. "I'd go mad without my work, so who am I kidding?"

"Well, that's sorted then. No more talk of retirement. It's a dirty word as far as I'm concerned. And as for the heavy night, it's a long one so I won't bore you with the details."

"It'll involve a woman, bound to. You're something of a Casanova on the quiet, so I'm told," said the doctor.

"That's a bloody lie! I like women and I've had some unfortunate relationships, that's all. And you shouldn't listen to gossip — it'll all be exaggerated."

The pathologist laughed and gestured for him to sit down.

"Wish I had your misfortune, Tom. That Lydia of yours is lovely — and young too. You're a lucky man; don't know how you do it."

"Your Pat would kill you if she heard what you'd just said," Calladine warned him. "Me and Lydia, we've had a bit of a spat, hence the way I look. I had too much to drink and stayed out all night with a friend, and now Lydia's moved into Zoe's place."

"Well, at least you know where she is. Get a bunch of flowers, pile on the charm, she'll come back."

Yes, she probably would, but that was part of the problem.

"Anyway, enough of my love life, have you got anything else from the post-mortems, Doc? Did Rocco tell you about Doctor Ahmed and the walking stick theory?"

"Yes he rang me, Tom, and I think he may be right. It's the narrow track of the blade and the depth of penetration. As I said, it sliced into his heart and right through his aorta — the poor man had no chance. There would have been absolutely nothing anyone could have done for him; he'd have bled out in no time."

Calladine winced. Poor sod. What had he done to deserve that? he wondered. What injustice was their killer trying to right with that one?

"Forensics?"

"We fared a little better there. Julian is still looking at the hair from the wig and he's got something from the beaker he found on the common. Have a word with him before you leave and he'll give you an update."

"We could do with something to give us a clue on this one. I think our killer is working through a list. I also think the method of killing is significant."

"Are you saying that your killer has a sort of *bucket list* of victims?"

That wasn't a bad way of putting it. "Exactly that, Doc."

"People usually have a bucket list when they are coming up to a milestone, Tom. A list of things to achieve before a major birthday, or . . ." He paused thoughtfully for a moment. "Or before they die." He looked up at the detective. "Have you considered that one? That your killer may have a terminal illness — cancer for example? Perhaps he or she was even one of Doctor Ahmed's patients."

"We are looking into that too. Getting the information is the tricky bit — you know what hoops we have to jump through."

Hoops or not, it was imperative that they did some digging. A vengeful killer with a bucket list of people to get rid of — the Doc could have something there. It was certainly worth investigating. They could start with North, and see what might connect him with one of Ahmed's patients — someone with a grudge to settle.

"D'you fancy a pint later, in the Wheatsheaf? Give us a chance to relax and unwind a bit before we go home and face . . ." He grimaced. "Well, before *I* have to go back and face up to the Lydia thing," said Calladine.

"Okay, Tom, I'll see you in there about seven."

"Great, Doc. I'll look forward to it. I'll pop along and see Julian before I go. Anything else comes up, let me know."

"I will, Tom, and don't you overdo it. We may be wedded to the job but at our age we need to stay on top physically."

Calladine walked briskly along the corridor to Julian's lab. He felt better. Talking to Doc Hoyle and the realisation that the method of killing was important, had helped lighten his mood.

"DI Calladine!" Julian Batho said when the inspector entered his lab. "I was going to ring you," he told him with a rare smile on his face. "I've got DNA from the beaker. Albert North's, as we would expect, and A.N. Other. They must both have drunk whiskey from it. North's DNA is on record but we don't have a match on the database for the other, I'm afraid. But come the day when you drag someone in. Then we'll see."

"That's great, Julian; I'm sure it'll pay dividends. Did any of the uniform boys or the scenes of crime people find anything that would suggest a break-in?"

"No, and we checked the place thoroughly. The killer must have been let in. Do you know whether anything was taken from the house?"

"No, but I don't think the motive was robbery. We've found someone who knew the doctor well. We're going to get her to look around his house and see if anything is missing. We'll try to get a DNA sample from her too."

"If you get anything, bring it in and I'll see what I can find."

* * *

He had walked to the hospital. It wasn't far from the nick and although the weather was still cold it wasn't raining and the fresh air would do him good — help clear his head. He intended to walk back to Ruth's and pick up his car. Oh, and coincidentally his route would take him past Amaris Dean's shop. Hopefully he'd find she was free.

He'd left the box there this morning. He'd not meant to, but being tired and still slightly the worse for the drink of the night before, he'd forgotten all about it. He wondered whether she would have opened it.

The shop was empty and Amaris was stacking shelves behind the counter.

"Hello," he greeted her sheepishly. "Thanks for last night and I'm sorry I crashed out like that on your sofa. It's not what I'm usually like, really."

She turned and gave him that smile; the one that had the power to make him go all boyish. Her long dark brown hair was loose and flowing over her shoulders. She looked so young, so lovely.

"It wasn't a problem, Tom. You were troubled. You're still troubled," she said coming closer and placing her hand on his arm. "Coffee? A chat, maybe?" she suggested. "I'm a good listener."

He checked his watch. Mid-morning; why not?

"Okay. Do you want me to mind the shop while you make it?"

She walked over to the door and turned the sign to 'closed.' "Not necessary. We'll take our coffee upstairs. You left your tin box here — I've got it safe for you."

She took him upstairs to her flat. It was warm, cosy and smelled of the same incense she'd been burning in the shop.

"Sit, relax and I'll put the coffee on." She reached over to a set of shelves and handed him the box. "I haven't peeked, I promise you, though I was tempted. It has a strange aura. It holds a secret that's made you afraid."

She was right on that score. But he wasn't just frightened, he was terrified. She could have looked, Calladine reasoned, then she'd know the secret. But had she? Could he believe her? He placed the box on a small table in front of the sofa.

"Amaris!" he called through to her. "Sorry I came here like this, but I wanted to thank you, and to retrieve my box."

"Call me Amy," she said, startling him as she came back into the sitting room with a tray of coffee. "Amaris is my business name — my Wicca name. Amy Dean is what's on all my official documents, and it's what my friends call me."

"Amy . . ." He pondered this for a moment. "I can understand an Amy — it's Amaris that scares the life out of me."

She laughed and put the tray down in front of them.

"What is it that scares you about my name, Tom?"

"Well, you, the whole package. The things you do — the stuff you seem to know."

"But I do know things, I can't help the way I am, can I?" She shrugged. "But you mustn't be afraid. I want us to be friends. Nothing I know can hurt you." Amy sat down beside him and kissed his cheek. "Do you have a woman in your life, Tom?"

Now he felt really nervous, and coughed, clearing his throat. He'd no idea where this was going.

"Don't you already know the answer to that?" he asked lightly. "With all your talents, I mean."

"I sense a complication — emotion but also distrust. Whoever you are with is not the woman for you and I think you are just beginning to realise that."

He shook his head. "In that case, I suppose the only answer I can give is — perhaps," he said throwing his arms in the air.

She laughed. "That makes no sense. Perhaps is not an answer, so I will ask instead — are you in love with anyone?"

Now that he could answer — no he wasn't. He'd been infatuated with Lydia, flattered by her interest in him, but it wasn't love. He shook his head.

"See, in that case you're free, emotionally free. Free perhaps to have dinner with me tonight?"

"You want me to take you out?"

She was smiling at him. That pretty mouth of hers, what was it saying, and what was she hinting at?

"If you wish." She paused, and her eyes were flashing him messages he didn't understand. "Or we could eat here, order something in." She took his hand in hers. "I would prefer that. I make no bones about my needs, Tom, and I'm sorry if my openness makes you uncomfortable, but I want to make love with you. I've wanted you since the moment you first walked into my shop."

Calladine was stunned. Amaris Dean wanted him! Wanted him in the *biblical way* as his mother would have said.

He pulled his hand free and a shiver ran through him. He'd no idea what to say to her, what to do. Had she sensed the desire in him?

"Well, Tom?" She took hold of his hand again. "Do you want to come here tonight and make love to me? I think you do. I touch your hand and I can sense it."

He looked at her face. That smile still lingered and those amazing eyes were twinkling with amusement. She knew. She knew damn well what she was doing to him. She probably knew too, how much he was attracted to her. He nodded. His mouth was too dry to speak.

"I'm a very open person and I'm sorry if it offends you, Tom. I have had many lovers, I've never married and I don't have children. I am wary of close emotional attachments — you see, they drain me. That might not be what you want to hear but you need to know before we start this. I want you to be under no illusions about what you're getting into."

She was very honest. Wary of emotional attachments — what was that supposed to mean? And what if he became emotionally attached?

"We'll see how it goes," he managed to mumble.

"Drink your coffee and take two of these. They'll make you feel better." She handed him two tablets.

"Some weird potion, are they?"

"Paracetamol," she replied, suppressing a giggle. "You have a hangover and I want you fresh for later." Then she leaned closer and kissed his mouth hard.

* * *

Calladine picked up his car and drove back to the nick. All this personal stuff was really messing with his head. First Eve Walker, or Buckley — and now Amaris, or Amy, Dean were whizzing around in his mind. It was all interfering with his thought processes where the case was concerned. He needed his wits about him.

But he couldn't forget what Amy Dean had just said to him. The way she'd spoken and her openness about what she wanted kept going round and round in his head. He should be flattered. He could hardly believe his luck — she wanted him, wanted him physically. And he wanted her too — but what to do about Lydia? She wouldn't just pat his arm and let him go. She'd be outraged that he was seeing another woman, and she'd retaliate. He shuddered. That woman had a mean temper.

There was a lot at stake here. And hadn't he already arranged to meet up with the doc in the Wheatsheaf? If he saw Amy then he'd have to cry off, but if he wriggled out of seeing her then what could he use as an excuse? She'd see right through him.

When he got back, Ruth and Rocco were still out. Joyce had her head glued to her computer screen and a tall man with blondish hair was leaning over Imogen as they both studied the contents of a file. Calladine looked at him quizzically for a moment or two. Who was this?

"Guv, er, DI Calladine!" Imogen called out when she saw him. "Come and join us!"

"I'll just dump my stuff!" he called back, indicating his office. He had to lose the coat but most of all he had to lock the box safely away in his desk drawer. Then he went back into the main office to meet Imogen's guest.

"This is DI Greco," she told Calladine with a big smile.

So this was the new detective who was causing such a stir at Oldston. The one who seemed to be making quite an impression on Imogen too.

"DI Stephen Greco," offered the man, holding out his hand.

Calladine shook it warmly. "Tom Calladine. Nice to meet you, Steve. I've heard a little about you already — putting them to shame over there I'm told."

"It's Stephen," he corrected, expressionless. "A fresh pair of eyes, you know how it is. I've looked over one or two outstanding cases and spotted things that hadn't been seen before.

Upset a couple of the old timers but I can't help that. I'm not here to make friends."

His attitude made that obvious enough. Calladine felt as if he'd had his wrist slapped over the name thing. Ruth had said that Greco was a bit of a loner and meticulous in his approach. Seems she was right. His colleagues must be worn down with his constant rechecking of the evidence. But if he got results, well, that's what mattered.

The effort and the attitude had evidently paid off. Calladine guessed he was in his mid-thirties, and he was already a DI. But if he really was ambitious, then he'd need to work on his social skills.

"That's not a local accent," Calladine remarked.

"I transferred from East Anglia — Norfolk," he bestowed a rare smile upon Calladine. "But villainy is villainy wherever you go."

"Norfolk. Flat with cornfields. I went there once on a boating holiday."

"I would never have left but the job demands it." He chose to ignore Calladine's attempt at more personal conversation. "If you want to get on, that is."

"Got your family with you?"

Greco merely nodded. A story there, Calladine decided.

"Your DC here has really got something," he said bringing the conversation back to the case. "She's spotted the obvious clue that my lot missed entirely. Look — both mothers of the missing girls had Facebook accounts and both were befriended by the same person at more or less the same time. This person who calls herself *Gail*."

Calladine didn't do Facebook so he'd no idea how this *friendship* thing worked.

"People simply ask to be your friend. If you accept then they can see what you put out there — text, photos, everything," Imogen explained, knowing he'd be baffled. "Stalking has never been easier." This was said with far too much flippancy for comfort.

"Why would people do that?" Calladine didn't understand. "Why would you let a complete stranger into your life like that and give them access to family photos? Do we know who this Gail is?"

"No," Greco replied. "And don't be misled. Gail is most likely a man masquerading as a woman. The profile they've set up is scanty at best and there's no proper photo, just a cartoon avatar."

He might as well be speaking in a foreign language.

"So you think 'Gail' is a man, but you've no proof?" That didn't sound like the Greco he'd heard about.

"Experience, Inspector," Greco assured him. "This person is looking for small children, particularly blonde-haired girls between four and six years old. Both Isla Prideau and Leah Cassidy fit the profile."

"So how do we catch the bastard?"

Calladine groaned inwardly as Stephen Greco shot him a look that plainly said he disapproved of such language. He'd have to work with this sod from time to time. Just what he needed.

"We find out who the account belongs to — really belongs to. We trace the service provider and then the IP address. I'll get on with it and keep you posted."

He turned to Imogen. She got a smile, Calladine noticed. "I'm grateful for your help. Don't worry, we'll get this one. The odds are stacking up against him now."

"Hold on, Inspector. Isla Prideau is our case. She disappeared from our patch and for all we know this Gail person operates from Leesworth too."

There was no way Calladine was simply going to let this new guy run off with his case. Clever though he might be Greco needed to learn some manners.

"This is no time to get parochial, DI Calladine. The girls need finding and you don't have the time or the resources, so be sensible. I'll continue the investigation and keep you informed." And with that, he left the station.

Calladine disliked the man extremely. He was pushy and he seemed to think no one else was as capable as he was. Well, he'd just have to learn.

"Imogen, set up our own incident board for the missing girls — stick on everything we've got."

"Won't that be stepping on toes, sir?"

"Too bloody right it will, but I'm not bothered. Are you?"

# CHAPTER 11

"If there's anything you or Jane don't want just sell it on," Harriet suggested. "Make a bob or two. I'm sure you've no objection to that, have you, Gordon?"

They were standing in Lessing's kitchen. Harriet was sipping on the mug of hot coffee he'd just handed her. He hadn't joined her but instead was looking through a pile of letters. He was in his shirtsleeves and lightweight trousers. Dressed like that, he'd soon get very cold in that cellar of his.

"It's good of you to bring them over," he conceded, looking up. "Jane will be very grateful that you thought of her. She's a sentimental girl." He smiled.

She'd have got that from her mother, Harriet thought. She doubted Lessing had ever had a sentimental or compassionate thought in his entire life. Harriet wondered if she could have found it in her heart to forgive him if she hadn't been going to die. She shuddered. What he'd done to Sybil was bad enough, but the children — that was something else, and he'd been at it for ages. The gang he worked for were clever; they arranged for children to be taken from many different localities, the UK, the continent, and so far no one had joined up the dots. Harriet read the local papers. She knew two kids had gone missing from around here, and she had no doubt that Lessing was responsible. No, she could never forgive the cruel bastard, not if she lived to be a hundred.

"I've left the stuff in a box in the boot of my car," she lied. "I'll get it for you later. Could I have a look at what props you've got first?"

"Sure — everything's downstairs in the cellar. I keep meaning to sort it out, exhibit some of the pieces properly in the spare room upstairs, but I never seem to get round to it."

"You've certainly got plenty of room," she said, looking around. "The house must seem very empty without . . . well, without Sybil, and with Jane being away at college such a lot."

"I get by." He smiled. "Nothing else I can do, is there?"

Who was he kidding? The way things were now would suit him perfectly. There was no one to bother him or interrupt his pursuits. But it would work in her favour because no one would miss him — not for a while anyway.

Gordon Lessing lived in a huge house on the outskirts of Leesdon. It stood on its own in a large garden bounded by a six foot stone wall. It was a perfect place in which to get forgotten — and that was exactly what was going to happen. Once she got him down those cellar steps he wouldn't come up again. Gordon Lessing would breathe his last in the cold and dark, just like her sister. In abject agony.

"How are you doing anyway? You don't look so good; the treatment is it?"

"Yes, chemo is wretched, but the prognosis is good," she lied.

He gave a nod and put his mail back on the dresser and the empty mug in the sink.

"Come on, then, we'll take a look," he said, leading the way. "It's all been down there for ages. Everything's a bit old and dusty, and you'll have to take it away yourself in your car," he told her. "So don't go choosing anything too big."

Harriet clutched her shopping bag tight as she carefully made her way down the steep, stone steps. She didn't want to fall. He'd put a light on but the enclosed space still looked dark and there was a musty smell. Obviously not much fresh air got in here.

"Where do we start?" Harriet asked looking at the array of different sized boxes piled up all over the floor. "Do any of these contain costumes?"

"There's some over there." He pointed to a long wooden trunk. "I can't vouch for the condition but with a wash they should be fine. The boxes in that far corner have some magician's tricks in them — worth a look, take what you want from them."

"Do you have a torch, Gordon? Even with the light on it's still difficult to see."

He was lurking near the steps — she wanted him to come in and help. She needed him in the centre of the room, where there was a large free area on the floor. That's where he'd lie when she'd finished with him, unable to move or to summon help. She placed her bag down beside the trunk, making sure the zipper along the top was fastened tight. The bag contained everything she'd need to keep him in here, so she didn't want him peeking.

"This trunk is heavy. Could you give me a hand?"

Finally he was beside her. He handed her a large torch in a heavy metal case as he prepared to help — just what she needed.

"I'm expecting an important call," he explained, placing his mobile phone on a shelf. "My business phone. I need to keep it handy. I could have somewhere to go at short notice — a new customer."

The two girls? she wondered. The icy cold was making her feel sick; nonetheless she'd have to keep up the act.

"There's some great stuff in here — the theatre company will be thrilled. It's very good of you to let us borrow them, Gordon," she trilled. "D'you think you could pull it out from the wall so I can get a better look?"

He bent over, grabbing the edge of the trunk. Now she had him. He was overweight, out of condition. The act of bending down rendered him off balance. He was hunkered down on his toes fishing around in the trunk. One blow and he'd be on the ground.

Harriet gripped the torch tight and raised it high. She'd get one shot at this. Lessing might be fat but he was a big man and stronger than her. If she failed then he'd have her. If that happened it would be her lying cold and forgotten down here.

With all the strength she could muster Harriet brought the torch crashing down against his head. He wobbled for a moment and then fell heavily to the floor on his side. He wasn't quite out of it, more stunned, so she didn't have long.

Harriet hit him again, this time a lot harder. Rage made her strong. The thing fell apart in her hand. He groaned and rolled onto his back — perfect.

She kicked out and hit him in the shins. She hated this man with a passion. Although it had been quite a blow, Harriet wasn't that strong, so he'd most likely come round again soon. She took a cable tie, a strong thick one, from her bag and fastened both his wrists together. He mumbled something, his body jolting as he tried to move. Harriet stood back, staring at the injured man. The only way to ensure he couldn't escape was to do his legs. She had to make him immobile.

She took the rope from her bag and bound his ankles together. It was done. She had him. It was just a shame that he didn't realise what was about to happen to him.

Harriet hummed to herself as she picked through the boxes looking for something to use on his legs. She needed something to hit him with. Poor Sybil had suffered with a broken leg for days before she was found. The same fate must befall him. It was the least she could do now — so she needed to find something heavy to hit his knees with.

*Do it*, the voice urged. *Do it now before he tries to escape. You'll never get another chance like this — take it!*

The voice was such a comfort — always on her side. Harriet looked around and noticed a crowbar lying amongst a pile of rusting tools. She picked it up, and it sat cold and heavy in the palm of her hand. She could do this. She had to do this; the voice demanded it.

Harriet raised the thing high with both hands. She aimed for his right kneecap and then closed her eyes.

Despite her weakened state the blow was strong with the hate behind it, and it landed with a dull sort of thud on his leg. She heard the thud and then a crack, and the room was alive with his shrieks as Gordon Lessing screamed in agony.

"Stop! What the fuck . . . ?" His garbled words were intermingled with gasps of pain. "Let me go! Come on, woman, have you gone mad?" He screamed again, and Harriet smiled. The pain must be unbearable.

She could see blood seeping through his trousers and there was a small pool forming on the floor where he lay. He was still yelping and swearing.

"Shush, Gordon, you need to listen to me. You're injured quite badly and I don't think you're going to make it. In fact I know you're not going to make it." She smiled down at him.

His terrified shriek nearly deafened her.

"Whatever this is about, we can sort it." He shot the words at her between gasps for breath.

"This is for Sybil." Her face wore a look of satisfaction as she took the crow-bar to his other knee.

Then Gordon Lessing lost consciousness. Harriet took a long silk scarf from the costumes box and wrapped it tight around his mouth. She was exhausted. All her strength had gone into the effort and the hate. She needed to rest now. She'd come back later to make sure he was still suffering.

But she'd done it, and it was no more than he deserved, the heartless bastard. She felt nothing — no pity, no remorse. Why was that? She wasn't a killer.

It was the illness. The cancer had not only eaten away at her body but it had also corroded all inhibition and all conscience. She could kill without guilt. What a power that was, she realised with a sudden rush of joy.

*The phone, Harriet, take his phone*, the voice urged. Good idea. She doubted he'd be able to reach it, but she shouldn't take any chances. Snatching it from the shelf, she put it in her bag.

# CHAPTER 12

"I've got something, sir," Imogen told Calladine excitedly. "Jayden North — you know, Albert North's nephew — he found the body on the common? Well, he's awaiting trial for breaking into Tariq Ahmed's car. Apparently he was looking for drugs."

Now that was something, but what did it mean? If the boy had a beef with Doctor Ahmed what did that have to do with his uncle ending up dead on the common?

"Bring him in," Calladine decided. "Take Rocco with you when he comes back."

"They've just pulled into the car park. I'll get my coat."

It might be nothing but it was odd nonetheless. What it meant, Calladine could only guess at. But it was a link, and the only one they had, between the North family and Ahmed.

"You should have come — she's nice," Ruth said, sticking her nose around his door.

"You know why I couldn't and it's nothing to do with you know what. Did she say anything, in front of Rocco, I mean?"

Ruth gave him one of her looks and shook her head.

"It's difficult to say whether she knows or not. She didn't seem surprised to see us and she was perfectly happy to talk.

She did admit that they were having an affair, she and the good doctor. It was a secret — apparently Ahmed was coy about announcing it to their colleagues. Samantha Hurst is a cool cookie though. She showed little emotion and certainly didn't strike me as being devastated by her lover's death."

"Imogen and Rocco have gone to bring Jayden North in. He broke into Ahmed's car looking for drugs," he told her. "I'm sat here trying to piece it together but I can't make the leap between that and the two deaths."

"Perhaps you shouldn't try — perhaps there is no link and it's simple coincidence."

"I don't believe in coincidence, as you well know."

Just at that moment Calladine's mobile rang. It was his daughter, Zoe.

"What's going on with you and Lydia?" she began, without even a 'hello.' "Only she's been stuck on our sofa crying her heart out since this morning and I haven't a clue what to do with her."

"I don't know what you think I can do about it. She walked out on me. It's not my fault if I don't come up to expectations. It was her decision to leave — I didn't tell her to go or anything. She's in a bad mood, that's all. She'll come round."

"You really are a piece of work where women are concerned," said Zoe. He wondered if she'd been talking to Ruth. "Bad mood my . . . well, you know what I mean. You've done something, said something, and whatever it is, you've really upset her."

"She'll sort herself out, you'll see. Lydia's tough. She doesn't need me, not really."

"Come on, what's happened? Because it's plain that something has."

"It's work, that's all. It gets in the way. She wants to do things and I can't. I'm up to my eyes in a big case at the moment — late hours, not much fun, you know how it is."

"So what do I do with her? She's mooching about our house like a lost soul. Can't you come and get her? Buy her something, take her out tonight?"

"Can't tonight — like I said, things are heavy at work."

At that, he felt Ruth, who was still in his office, rap his arm. Damn the woman — she was worse than a conscience.

"Give her a bit longer — she'll be fine, I promise you."

"Okay, but if she's still here tomorrow then it's up to you. Got it?"

"We'll speak in the morning then."

Calladine put his mobile back in his jacket pocket and rubbed his neck. "Women! Always on my back, the bloody lot of them."

"Things heavy at work, my eye," Ruth scoffed. "Doesn't stop you chasing after Amaris does it? Lydia took care of you when you were ill — you owe her. At the very least she deserves more than the fobbing off that you've got planned."

"Perhaps I'll speak to her later on in the week. I'll leave her be for now."

"Wimp!" she retorted. "So who's going to interview the North lad?"

"Me and you, I reckon."

"Give me a couple of ticks to get straight."

"Take your time — they've only just left to bring him in."

Calladine poured himself a coffee from the pot in his office. Zoe was right and so was Ruth. He'd have to come clean sooner or later. He didn't love Lydia, and probably never had. He'd been infatuated, flattered by her attention. He could see that now and he wanted out. Now Amaris Dean . . . the very thought of her set his nerve ends tingling. He'd have to see how that went.

He downed the lukewarm liquid and went out into the main office. There were two incident boards directly in his line of vision — two dead men on one, and on the other, the two missing girls. They should be spending their time looking for the kids, who might still be alive. He didn't want to think about what their parents were going through. On the positive side, despite what he might think of the man personally,

Greco seemed like a smart cop. He was certainly more likely to find them than Thorpe was.

"Guv!" Ruth called out. "Jayden North — he didn't just do Doctor Ahmed's car. It seems he went on a bit of a spree and did about six of them in the 'Doctors only' car park." She handed him a copy of the charge sheet. "It's entirely likely that he's telling the truth and he'd no idea who the cars belonged to, and he really was simply looking for drugs."

She was probably right. Another dead end then.

"What do you want to do?"

"He's been interviewed once this week already, and he's out on bail until he goes back to court," he said looking at the sheet again. "A lot of stuff was found on him but no drugs. He took a laptop, a phone and some cash. I don't think it'll get us anywhere but I'll have a word anyway." He thought for a moment. "I can do this on my own so would you make arrangements to take Doctor Hurst to Ahmed's house?" With that he left the office.

Rocco and Imogen were bringing a sheepish-looking Jayden North into the building as Calladine went down the corridor.

"Soft interview room," he instructed them. "Are you okay, Jayden? How are you doing — getting things sorted for Albert's send-off?"

"Me dad's seeing to it," he mumbled. "He's emptying the place. Council want the flat back quick."

Calladine led the way into the small room and indicated for Jayden to sit on one of the upholstered chairs.

"Imogen, you stay here with me. Rocco, go up to the office. Ruth wants you to go with her to meet Doctor Hurst."

"Sorry to drag you in, lad." He smiled at him.

Imogen stood at the back wondering why the inspector was being so friendly.

"I know you're waiting to go to court for the car robbery and that you'll have your say then, but I have a couple of questions, if that's okay?"

The boy shrugged. His eyes were fixed on his empty hands lying in his lap.

"Did you know that one of the cars belonged to a Doctor Tariq Ahmed?"

He shook his head.

"I'm asking because Doctor Ahmed was murdered earlier this week."

At that Jayden North's head sprang up and his eyes filled with fear as he regarded the detective. "You can't pin that on me. I had nothing to do with it. I didn't even know whose car I was robbing."

Calladine shook his head, opened his mouth to reassure the boy, but he butted in.

"You won't make it stick. You lot can never make anything stick against us Norths. Look at all that stuff with Uncle Albert — didn't make that stick, did you? Evidence or not you still didn't have enough to stitch him up for murder!"

This really threw Calladine, not because of the boy's anger, but because of what he'd said.

"Your uncle was had up for murder?"

"You bloody well know he was. But you lot, you made mistakes," he smirked. "You got it wrong and he got off."

"When was this, Jayden?"

"I'm not saying. I'm not saying nothing anymore. I know my rights and I want to go." He stood up and made for the door.

"Thanks for coming in." Calladine nodded at Imogen to show him out.

So Albert North had once been accused of murder. Calladine hadn't known that, but he certainly needed to know all about it now. He wanted to know who the victim was and when the crime had occurred. He hurried back to the main office and collared Ruth before she left.

"He's not saying anything except that he had no idea who owned the cars he robbed. But he did get rattled when I told him that Ahmed had been murdered."

"Did he make the connection with his uncle? You didn't tell him did you? Not even the press have that little snippet yet."

"No, of course I didn't tell him. But Jayden was positive that even if we did think he was involved we'd never make a case of it. Apparently Albert North was once accused of murder, and he got off. What do you think? Does it ring any bells?"

She shook her head. "Perhaps it was before my time."

"Not before mine though. I was here when North was the big cheese on the Hobfield. But I don't recall him being involved in anything as serious as murder."

"Imogen!" he called out. "Would you check that out? See if there's anything in North's record that even hints at murder. Joyce might have turned up something — she was on the task earlier."

"What about Samantha Hurst?" He turned to Ruth. "Will she cooperate? Give a DNA sample?"

"She was still working, sir. So we're meeting her at Tariq Ahmed's house in about an hour."

"Good. Get her talking. Once she's back in his house she might let something slip. Try to get an insight into their relationship and what was going on in their lives. Someone was interested enough in them — well him anyway — for this to have happened at all."

# CHAPTER 13

Samantha Hurst was already waiting beside her car in the driveway.

"I have to be back within the hour," she told them.

Ruth could tell from her face that she was annoyed at having to be here. She probably thought she had better things to do. Samantha Hurst was tall; she had long legs and looked elegant in a plain red wool coat with a fur collar and knee-high boots. Her hair was dark and cut into a swingy chin-length bob.

"We're mad busy trying to fill in all the gaps since, well, since Tariq." Her eyes dipped and her mouth pulled into a line. Ruth couldn't read the woman. Was that a look of emotion or irritation at the inconvenience?

"This won't take long," Ruth assured her. "We'd like you to have a walk around inside. See if you can spot if anything is missing or has been moved since you were last here."

Ruth nodded at the uniformed PC standing on the doorstep and he unlocked the door.

Samantha walked straight into the sitting room, giving the closed kitchen door a quick glance as they passed. "Is that where . . . ?"

"Yes. Doctor Ahmed was murdered in there. If it's any consolation, it would have been quick. A matter of seconds, the pathologist said."

"It isn't. Any consolation, I mean. Everyone who knew him thought he was difficult: an oddball who didn't show much emotion. But we had something, and I'll miss him," she admitted. "We were serious about our relationship. We got on socially and professionally, and I liked him a lot."

"Had you been together for long?"

"Why? What difference does that make? The time doesn't matter . . . we had discussed a future together. Not at once — we both wanted to give it a little longer, get on with our careers first," she disclosed. "He and I thought we had plenty of time to do anything we wanted." She shook her head. "Now that's all gone and I have to rethink."

"I'm very sorry."

"We were together about six months. At the beginning we used to argue about everything. Back then I really didn't like him much at all. I couldn't understand the way he was. Why he always seemed so cold and detached from the job. Then one day, when we were dealing with a particularly sad case, I got it. I finally understood." She smiled grimly. "It's a hard job, telling people they're going to die, and with Tariq his brusque manner was his way of protecting himself from all the misery he had to inflict."

"I see. Underneath all that top medic veneer, he was really a softie."

"I wouldn't go that far, but he wasn't the man our colleagues at work thought of him as."

"Mrs Hurst, can I ask about your movements on the night he was killed?"

Ruth had to ask, but as Samantha Hurst turned and regarded her closely for a few moments, she saw the incredulity on her face. "You think I could have done that to him?" Her voice faltered.

"You were here, we know that. But what I need from you is a timeline. I need to know when you arrived, when you left, and where you went afterwards. Also, would you be prepared to do a DNA test?"

She shook her head. "A little over the top if you ask me. Anyway I can clear up the question of my whereabouts very simply." She shrugged. "I came to give him something, stayed about half an hour, long enough for a coffee and a sandwich, and then I went back to the hospital. What time was he killed?"

"Sometime after nine."

"In that case I can put your mind at rest. From seven forty-five to gone ten that night I was in theatre. You can check the rota, and there are at least a dozen witnesses to back me up."

Ruth was relieved. That meant Calladine could relax. His half-sister was not the murderer.

Rocco had stayed in the background. He was taking notes. Ruth would get him to check Samantha's alibi once they got back to the nick.

"It all seems much as it always is." Samantha Hurst walked around the room. "He has a safe in his bedroom. You should check that." She turned to face the detective, catching her off guard. "You're staring. What's wrong?"

Ruth shook her head, trying to make light of it. What could she say? She *had* been staring; the woman was Calladine's sister. Now she felt embarrassed. "Nothing," she replied hastily.

The doctor gave a smile and a nod but she had been right, Ruth had been looking for resemblances between her boss and his half-sister. She had the same dark hair, although his was now rapidly turning to grey. She also had the angular features, particularly the cheekbones. They must get that from their mother, she thought with a smile.

"Do you have children?" Ruth asked.

"Why? What's that got to do with anything?"

"I just wondered . . ." Ruth felt foolish for asking something so personal.

"But yes, I have a teenage son. Callum. You?"

"No, not yet," Ruth answered. "You've got your hands full, then."

"He's a good boy. To date he's not given me any cause for concern. He wasn't all that keen on Tariq though. Wouldn't talk to him or go out anywhere with us."

"Why was that?"

"He had some weird notion that he was betraying his dad. Richard Hurst and I might be separated, but he's still very much a part of Callum's life."

"I'll go upstairs and check the safe," Rocco interrupted. "Where is it?"

"It's in the master bedroom at the bottom of the large wardrobe."

"Odd place for a safe."

"Apparently it was there when Tariq bought the place, and it was far too heavy to move — so he used it. He kept a little money and some family jewellery in it, he kept the key in the teapot in the kitchen."

Minutes later Rocco was back. "It's all fine up there; nothing untoward with the safe."

"It doesn't look like anything was taken then," Samantha said. "But I can't understand why anyone would want to kill Tariq." She turned to have a last look around and walked towards a coffee table by the window. "The tickets have gone," she said suddenly, tapping the shiny surface. "That's what I brought round — two tickets for the art exhibition at the community centre on Friday. We were planning to go together. You can see from the walls that Tariq was something of a collector."

"Are you sure you put them there? Perhaps the doctor moved them," Ruth suggested. "Have a closer look, in the sideboard and the cupboards perhaps."

"He wouldn't move them because I told him not to. I didn't want him to lose them."

"I'll make a note of it," said Rocco.

"I can offer you something even more useful, Detective Constable. The tickets are all numbered and I made a note of ours," she said, looking inside her handbag. "I lost a pair of very pricey West End theatre tickets once, and ever since then I write down the details in case it happens again." She took out a notebook, ripped out a page and handed it to Ruth. "There. If anyone is foolish enough to use them, you'll have got the evil bastard who killed Tariq."

\* \* \*

"Why the missing kids board?" Long was annoyed. He'd walked into the incident room and seen that the murder board had been shunted to one side so that the missing kids were centre stage. And to make matters worse Calladine was standing gazing at it as if he had nothing better to do. "I told you to hand the case over to Oldston. I hope you aren't wasting time, Inspector, not when you've got a double murder on your hands."

"Isla Prideau is our responsibility. I can't simply file the case away and trust Greco to sort it."

"But he will sort it. Mark my words, the man misses nothing."

"It's not about what he does or doesn't miss. The kids thing could be big. Have you considered that we could be seeing only a tiny bit of what's really going on nationwide?"

"You mean trafficking?"

"Exactly. Leesworth or Oldston could be a hub. We need to look deeper because if this is trafficking then it won't go away. They will be seasoned operators, and they'll take some catching."

"Leave it to Greco, Tom. Oldston has more resources. They have the city force on the doorstep and we've got enough to think about."

"It'll do no harm to keep the abductions live. I have a feeling that this case is going to need a lot more throwing at it than one keen detective who's had a bit of luck recently."

"It's more than luck. He's a damn good cop. He's been tipped to make DCI within the next couple of years. The minute there's an opening he'll be in."

"Working in an area like Oldston is very different from rural Norfolk — so we'll see."

Long shook his head. Calladine was at it again. He should give him a good bollocking for insubordination or something, but the truth was he didn't have the energy. Now he knew why the job had defeated Jones. The post of DCI in this nick was a right pig and the sooner he could ditch it and get back to normal the better. And when that happened he'd have Calladine on his side again. They had got on before— after a fashion. They had certainly never crossed swords like they had recently.

"Perhaps I shouldn't be so critical but I can't help it. This is missing kids, Brad, little kids at that. They can do nothing to defend or help themselves. They need finding and the bastards that took them need locking up."

"It'll happen, Tom, just give Greco time. You can't take on the world; you're just one man. Besides he's a lot younger than you."

He ducked as Calladine threw a small stapler at him.

"I only hope he's as good as you all say, because if he isn't, it could cost those kids their lives."

"I know you're concerned but we're stuck with him. Who knows, he might even end up becoming our DCI. I can't stay *acting* forever and now that I've had a taste, I wouldn't want the job."

"D'you really think that's a serious possibility?"

"I heard a rumour, nothing more. But you have to admit, given his record, it sounds plausible. It's quite possible that Greco could end up here at Leesdon. But heaven help us all if he does!"

\* \* \*

"Sir!" Imogen called out as she came into the office. "Whatever we've got on North from the past isn't held electronically. It's on paper records, and it's now in the archive. You know as well as I do that there're two rooms full of the stuff. We could do with knowing when this was — even the year would help."

"Jayden wasn't very forthcoming. The mere mention of murder got his back up." He looked at Imogen. "But you might get somewhere. He might soften if you talk to him."

She was closer to Jayden's age and pretty. It was worth a shot. They were working against the clock on all fronts so it couldn't hurt.

"Okay, I'll have a ride around the Hobfield and see if I can track him down."

"Don't go on your own. If Rocco's not back when you leave, then take a uniform with you."

Calladine hurried back into his office. His phone was ringing.

"Dad, it's Zoe," his daughter began. "She's leaving. Lydia got her stuff together and she says she's going for a train. If you don't do something — now — then you could lose her for good."

On top of everything else. Just what he needed.

"Has she said anything? Where's she's going, what her plans are? I thought she was staying with you. Why all the sudden rush?"

"I've no idea what's going on. She said something to Jo about a job coming up, but she didn't say where."

He could do without this. He was up to his ears in police work, and what he didn't need right now was a domestic crisis.

"Okay — I'll be with you in ten minutes. Try and keep her there."

He grabbed his coat and car keys; a quick word to Imogen and he was gone. Zoe and Jo, her partner, lived on a small housing estate between Leesdon and the bypass. It had about thirty or so houses, mostly detached and expensive, all built on the site of a once rambling old pub and its car park. How things had changed. Calladine had no idea why, but

Leesworth had become a fashionable place to live in recent years. Builders were falling over themselves to get their hands on any pocket handkerchief of land that became available.

Zoe waved to him from the window and opened the front door.

"She's in the kitchen," his daughter hissed at him. "For God's sake do something with her. I'm rapidly running out of patience with the woman."

Calladine strode down the hallway and stood in the kitchen doorway. Lydia was seated on a high stool sipping coffee with Jo. The two women were deep in conversation.

"You're too late," Lydia sniffed at him. "I've just been telling Jo — I'm going and you can't stop me."

"Going where? Why the hurry, why all the drama, and why am I the last to know?"

"Because I've had enough, and I finally see you for what you are, Tom Calladine."

"And what's that?"

"A boring workaholic detective with no time for his lover, his family or his friends — that is, if you have any! And don't argue the point, because you know I'm right. You've hardly spent any time at home since you went back to work. You don't love me. You don't need me at all, do you? Not really, if you're honest."

"I thought we were okay," he replied lamely. What else could he say? What was it she expected from him, and where the hell had this come from so suddenly?

"Oh, we are — provided I don't ask for anything, or want some affection."

He didn't like the sound of that at all. He considered that he gave Lydia a whole heap of affection, and regularly too. "So what is it you want?" He was floundering in a quagmire of emotions. Lydia, Amy, they were spinning around in his head, each face rising into his mind's eye in turn. One was a woman he was used to, and one was an unknown quantity — who did he want?

"I want you to spend time with me, take me out, and help me with my work," she implored. "I've asked you till I'm blue

113

in the face, but still you hang back. You know how much I need your cousin's story, and you could help me get it, you know you could. He'd speak to you, he'd open up, I know he would, you're family."

This again! That was all he needed. Calladine was sick to the back teeth of her constant harping on about Fallon.

"Well, that's where you're wrong because he's not," he retorted sharply. It was out before he could stop it.

"Not what?"

"Family. He's no relation to me at all." Three pairs of eyes swung his way. "And he'll know it soon enough, so I'll be nothing but another nosey cop as far as he's concerned."

Zoe stood staring at him with her hands on her hips.

He flashed an apologetic look at her. She'd know he wasn't lying. She'd know from the pain on his face and the way he spoke that he meant it.

"I thought Ray Fallon was your cousin, Dad."

"So did I, but he isn't." He ran a hand through his short hair. Now he'd done it. "Look, I can't explain now. I've only known myself for a little while, but put simply, Freda wasn't my birth mother, hence Fallon's not my cousin."

So there it was, out in the open, the bombshell. Soon the questions would start — the difficult ones he had no answer for. He couldn't do this, not yet, it was too soon. But he'd have to give Zoe something at least.

"Fallon is the son of Freda's sister," he explained to the stunned faces. "So if Freda's not biologically related to me, then neither is Fallon." He gave them a small smile. "Personally I think it's something to be grateful for."

His last comment fell on deaf ears as the expected barrage of questions erupted all around him — mostly from Zoe. He didn't want this. It wasn't how it should be. He'd wanted to tell Zoe privately, gently, but now it was too late. He'd never felt so uncomfortable in his entire life. It was the wrong time, he thought to himself again. And then he turned on his heel and left them to it, letting the front door slam shut behind him.

# CHAPTER 14

Harriet Finch slept for most of the afternoon. The moment she woke the memories of her morning's work flooded back. A mix of horror and satisfaction made her feel slightly high. How could she do the most awful things and then sleep like an infant? This was not like the old Harriet at all.

She'd get up now and make some tea and then she'd wait until it was dark and go back and check on Lessing. She'd take her car, but park it in the next road. Harriet didn't want the neighbours to see it parked on Lessing's drive. Twice in one day might cause tittle-tattle.

Harriet felt happier than she had in weeks. She sang to herself as she pottered about the house. She had a shower and put on the long dressing gown and fluffy slippers that were a present from her friend Nesta. She should ring Nesta and tell her about the tickets for the art exhibition. It would mean spoiling the surprise, but she didn't want her arranging something else for her birthday. She'd miss Nesta, Harriet thought with a smile. She'd been a good friend, always there when she needed her.

Suddenly Lessing's mobile made the most horrendous noise. It sounded like one of those vicious dogs barking — very apt. Harriet had put the thing on her coffee table in the sitting room and forgotten about it. She stared at the bright screen as it barked away and vibrated around on the shiny wooden surface. The name *Yuri* flashed across the screen, illuminated in blue. She closed her eyes. There was only one man Lessing knew who was called Yuri.

She felt sick again. It was him, Lessing's contact with the traffickers. Harriet was shaking. Her nerves were jangling and causing her head to ache. Should she tackle him about it? Should she make Lessing talk to her, perhaps even record a confession for the police?

Harriet picked up the phone. It wasn't like hers; it was one of those that did everything with a touch screen. Hers was old, used only for phone calls and texting — not that she ever texted anybody. She swiped her finger across the screen — what now? She had a laptop, so she wasn't completely ignorant about technology.

"Hello," she practically whispered.

"Lessing, I want Lessing."

"He's been taken ill," she told him. "Can I take a message?"

The phone went dead.

She moved her finger around the screen looking for anything that might give her clue as to what to do next. *Gallery* — that would be photos she reasoned, tapping hard. What she saw next made her jump and throw the thing to the ground. Nothing but images of children, dozens of them — taken in parks, in the street, with their families. Why?

Harriet knew very well why. She was being stupid — they were only photos, snaps, they couldn't harm her. She bent down and picked the thing up again. It was the knowledge of what Lessing and his cohorts would do with those images that bothered her. They would use them to source likely candidates.

Then she saw them — the two little girls, both in school uniforms. They could only be four or five years old and her heart immediately went out to them. They were the girls she'd seen in the newspaper, the missing girls from Oldston and Leesworth. That must mean that Lessing had lined them up to be taken too.

Gordon Lessing knew this man: Yuri. He had photos of the girls on his phone, so he was involved right up to his fat neck. He was a heartless, wicked bastard and he should suffer for his sins! Harriet was angry — she'd make him talk if it was the last thing she ever did. She desperately wanted to help those poor children. It would make up for some of the awful things she'd done over the last few days.

Harriet got dressed, but the anger and exertion had exhausted her again. She was getting weaker. Every day she could do less than the day before. *Slowly, girl*, she told herself, *take it slow. After tonight, after you've got what you want from Lessing you can relax, put your feet up — your work will be done.*

But would it? She bit her lip. The list was like a piece of elastic. It had started with the three, but now . . . it seemed that anyone who crossed her, who had ever argued with her in the past, was a candidate. Killing was addictive. The need to kill grew inside her every bit as fast as the cancer did. It was like drink or drugs — it was compulsive, and she revelled in it. Harriet had no idea what had possessed her recently but it was far too late to stop now, so she might as well enjoy herself. When she was finally ready to leave, she found her list and added the name *Yuri* to the bottom.

\* \* \*

Jayden North was not at home. The flat he had lived in with his father was in darkness and looked empty.

"We've driven round the estate three times already," the uniformed officer told Imogen with distinct irritation in his voice. "You know what these types are like — a dab hand at avoiding the law, the lot of them."

"He's got to surface at some stage," Imogen replied. "Pull up outside that tower block," she indicated. "We'll wait and watch for a while, see if he comes back."

The officer sighed and pulled into a parking space. "You're wasting your time, you know. He won't help you. The Norths are a bad lot, always have been.

"That's as might be, but I still need a word. It's important. Young Jayden is sitting on information that might help us crack the case we're working on."

The officer shook his head and tutted. "Madness, that's what it is, relying on a toerag like him. He'll not give you anything — he's a bad 'un — just like all the rest."

"Is this him?" Imogen asked, as a group of youths approached. "You know, I think it is — he was wearing that top earlier."

She hopped out of the car and made towards them. "Jayden!" she called out.

The group of lads he was with started whistling and whooping. The DC with her long blonde hair and shapely body made a striking impression. She was wearing jeans, a short fur-trimmed jacket and leather boots.

"What d'you want now?" He frowned at her, embarrassed at being accosted like this in front of his mates. "You're wasting your time cos I've got nowt to say, so bugger off."

"No way to talk to a lady," one of his cohorts interjected, pushing him to one side. "Where d'you find her? She's a right looker." He stood in front of Imogen and pulled heavily on a cigarette. "You don't want to bother with him, babe," he winked. "He's a muppet. You'd be much better off with a real man, like me." Then he blew smoke in her face, thrust out his denim clad pelvis and laughed with the rest of them.

Imogen was used to this kind of thing. She'd been to the Hobfield many times before and had met dozens like this one.

"Can I have a quiet word please, Jayden?" she asked, disregarding the banter and brushing her wind-blown hair from her face. "You're not in any trouble. It's just that something you said earlier got me thinking."

Jayden shrugged, his eyes scanning the ground beneath him. Imogen could hear the others laughing and ribbing him.

What the hell, it would do him no harm. Being swooped on by the police like this would give him a kudos he'd find a use for. It would help him up the pecking order in the gang he ran with.

"You do want us to catch whoever it was murdered your uncle, don't you?" Imogen asked quietly as she walked him away from the group. "Only you didn't seem keen to speak to us earlier and that's a shame because I think you know stuff that might help. We think Albert was killed in an act of revenge. We also think the way he was killed was significant."

"What d'you mean?" he asked.

Now she had his attention. Imogen knew that revenge was something he understood.

"You said something about him being implicated in a murder years ago. We don't mean to drag up unpleasant memories, but will you tell me about it, Jayden?"

"Not that again. I don't believe you, you're just stirring it, so why should I?"

"Because, like I say, it might help. It's just possible that his death is somehow connected to that incident. But since we don't know when it happened or who was involved we can't act. Your silence could be wasting us valuable time." Imogen was growing impatient. "I think you do know something but it's misplaced loyalty to your uncle that's stopping you telling me."

"Albert told me lots of stuff. But mostly he told me never to tell you lot anything."

"Nothing you tell us can harm your uncle now, Jayden. Albert was murdered; don't you want us to catch his killer?"

"It's complicated. I don't want to say too much."

"Anything you can tell us will help."

"He didn't do anything, whatever the police said. It wasn't him that burned that kid," Jayden insisted. "He told you lot all this at the time."

"What d'you mean — burned?"

"Set him alight, fried him to a crisp, what the fuck d'you think I mean?"

"Okay Jayden, no need to get all riled up. But you do see what I'm getting at? You found Albert — you saw what had been done to him."

* * *

Yes he had. The image of his uncle sitting stock still, his head all blackened and burned was one that would live with Jayden for a long time. He shuddered and looked at Imogen. The cop might have something, he reasoned, but he still wasn't going to tell her anything. If she was right, if this was deliberate, then the bastard that had done that to Albert needed fixing for good, and he was the one to do it.

"I only know what he told me, Uncle Albert, and that's all. He said you lot got it wrong — it wasn't him. You had a bloody good try at pinning it on him though," he scoffed. "But none of it stuck. A long time ago it was, before I was even born, so I can't help. Now piss off."

Imogen passed him her card. "If you think of anything, anything at all, or if you want to talk then ring me," she urged. "We want this killer caught every bit as much as you do, Jayden."

Jayden North doubted it. They wouldn't waste their time. They'd drop the whole thing after a bit — move on to something else. Albert had been a thorn in their side for years, so it would be a case of good riddance. He took the card, nodded and stuffed it in his pocket.

The youths watched the car pull away. Jayden said his goodbyes and broke away from the group. He had things to do now. Jimmy Finch, that had been the lad's name, and he had a mother still living in Leesdon. Albert had told him how angry the boy's family had been, and how they'd sworn to get him one day.

He smiled to himself. That blonde cop had done him a favour. He'd have to pay Mrs Finch a visit.

* * *

120

It was just after six in the evening when Harriet left her house. It was so dark she could sink into anonymity in the shadows. She had just sat down in the driver's seat of her car when Lessing's mobile rang. The noise frightened her. She hadn't planned for this; she should have turned the thing off. She took it from her bag — it was him again, Yuri.

Her stomach was flipping over with nerves. What to do?

"Hello," she rasped, "what d'you want?"

*Come on, you're not afraid. This is your chance to get this bastard,* the voice purred. *He's a villain, worse than that, he steals little girls. You can stop him. That would be a good way to finish this.*

The voice was right. If she was to get this man then she needed to talk to him, meet him even, scary as that prospect might be.

"I want what's mine."

His voice was deep with a thick accent. She didn't recognise it — possibly Romanian, something like that. Harriet could barely make out what he said.

"Lessing is holding some merchandise for me. I want it back, lady, so if you have any influence then tell him not to be stupid."

Merchandise! He was talking about two small children! Forget the fear; this one would be a real pleasure. It was good news because it meant that the girls were probably still alive and being held somewhere.

"He's ill, I told you." There was new confidence in her voice. "What merchandise? Perhaps I can help?"

"You know where he put it?"

No, she didn't, but she wouldn't tell Yuri that.

"Yes, of course. I'm his partner. We live together."

"Then we meet. You tell me where the goods are and all will be well. I have transport waiting. I must leave the country with the goods tonight." There was a long pause. "But if you cross me I will kill you. Then I'll kill Lessing. Do you understand?"

"There's no need to take that tone," she replied sharply. "It's not Gordon's fault he's been taken ill. He's in hospital, probably in theatre as we speak."

"My heart bleeds." He laughed humourlessly. "I want what's mine and I want it tonight."

"Tell me where to meet you."

"Oldston. You know the side street up by the library?"

"Yes."

"You go there tonight at eight. You take me to my merchandise. If all is correct, then I pay you and we go our separate ways."

"Sounds like a plan," Harriet said lightly.

"Describe yourself," he barked.

"I'm tallish with long red hair. I'm wearing a cream-coloured fur coat so you can't miss me, even in the dark," she lied. Now she had the edge. Harriet was pleased with herself. She was good at this. She'd recognise him but he wouldn't know her.

"Don't be late."

With that he was gone.

# CHAPTER 15

"God, I've had enough of today." Calladine leaned forward in his chair and rubbed the back of his neck. "Imogen got nowhere with Jayden North. He still won't tell us what he knows, stupid lad," he told Ruth wearily. "I'm supposed to be going round to see Amy — Amaris, but I can't face that either. I'm pooped. All I want is a warm fire, some food and a large scotch."

"Then you'll fall asleep, no doubt." She shook her head. "Dare I ask about Lydia?"

"Please don't. It was a disaster. We ended up rowing and I walked away. I let it slip about my mother too, in front of Zoe and Jo."

"It had to come out sooner or later, Tom."

"But not like that. I'm a bloody fool and no mistake. I reacted to Lydia's goading. She was going on and on about Fallon, and me having influence because he's my cousin. So out it came." He grimaced. "Not what I intended, but like you say, it's done now."

"Go home and get some rest, then tomorrow we can look at all this afresh." She waved her arm at the board in the adjoining office.

"I promised to have a drink with the doc." He checked his watch. "He'll be waiting for me in the Wheatsheaf. Don't fancy coming too, do you?"

"I suppose it'll do no harm. Jake has a parents' evening at school so the house will be empty." She checked her watch. "Half an hour, then, but when I order orange juice I don't want to hear any smart remarks from you. Remember, this is still a secret." She rubbed a hand over her belly. "And while we're on the subject I'll need an hour or so off tomorrow morning. We've got our first scan."

"Will you get a piccy?"

"Of course — and then I'll start to tell people. But for now, not a word."

The Wheatsheaf was busy for a Thursday. People were crowding around the bar and every table was full.

"Quiz night," Ruth remarked. "Popular too. Wonder what they offer by way of prizes?"

"Not much. It's all about getting one up on the other teams," Sebastian Hoyle said as he walked over to join them. "Good to see you, Ruth. You're looking well."

"Thanks, Doc. A girl has to try." She smiled back at him.

"Still seeing that chap of yours, teacher, isn't he?"

Ruth nodded and gave Calladine a warning glance. "Have you told your friend you won't be coming?" she asked him.

No, he hadn't. Calladine swore under his breath and took himself outside where it was quieter to give Amy a ring. "Sorted," he said, as he returned. "I've rearranged for tomorrow. With any luck I'll have got my head straight by then."

He was feeling better. Amy had seemed fine about it, and the relaxed atmosphere of the pub was calming him down. A couple of pints, a chat with the doc, and he could go home and chill properly.

"Case, Tom?" the doc asked, sipping on his pint.

"It's becoming a nightmare. We can't get any further forward. So far we've had two murders, both very different, but both by the same killer. We have a theory that it's about revenge, but that isn't getting us anywhere either."

"The bucket list of victims we were talking about?"

"You've discussed this?" Ruth asked.

"A little," the doc confirmed. "It strikes me that Tom could be right. Someone out there has a list and is out for revenge. So the method of killing is significant."

"Albert North's nephew has information but he won't talk."

"Information about what, Tom?" the doc asked.

"As you know, Albert was set alight. And apparently he was involved in something similar years ago but he got off — no proper evidence. A kid was left for dead and set alight but we don't know when and the case notes are in the archive. You know what that means," he said pulling a face.

"I hate the burnt ones," the Doc shuddered. "I know I'm a pathologist but they still make me queasy. You know, when his body came in and I started the PM, I remembered every single one I've ever done. I can't recall the names, but my first was a youth, years ago, and he was in a dreadful mess. Someone had done a right job on him. If I remember rightly we couldn't get much in the way of forensics. The senior investigating officer at the time had a right go — I remember that alright," he said with a sniff. "There was a court case but whoever they had in the frame walked. It was a long time ago, and there haven't been that many since. Could that have been Albert North?"

"Worth a look at. Can you remember the year — or even better, the name?"

"No, but I know I worked on the case. It was way back when I was just starting out. I'd done five years in general practice and was bored to tears. It was one of the first cases I was part of. I recall being scared to death."

"What about your records? Are they any easier to put your hands on than ours?"

"Sorry Tom, but no. Like yours they're archived away and on paper."

Ruth nudged Tom with her foot under the table. "Look who's just come in," she told them both.

It was Imogen and Julian Batho. They hadn't seen them sitting there and went straight to the bar. The forensic scientist had his arm around the blonde DC's waist.

"That pair looks very friendly," the doc noted with a smirk. "Anything I should know?"

Calladine watched the young couple for a few seconds. They were obviously enjoying each other's company — but then as Julian kissed Imogen's cheek, he noticed the three of them staring.

"We're busted," he said to Imogen, holding his hands in the air and walking towards them.

"You lot never come in here," he announced to the group, sounding decidedly miffed. "Too close to work you always said, Ruth."

"It was a last minute thing for me." She smiled. "It's these two who fancied a session and the closer the better so this one can walk home."

"So, you two," Calladine smiled. "Anything we should know?"

"Nothing you need to, Inspector," Julian replied, putting his arm back around Imogen's waist.

The detective constable looked a little embarrassed. Both Calladine and Ruth knew that Imogen didn't like being the subject of gossip.

"It's early days," she told them. "We all know what you lot are like so you can't blame me for keeping Julian to myself for a bit."

"Oh, we don't." Ruth nodded. "I'll lay odds we're all keeping a little something back."

"I'm not!" Calladine piped up.

"Only because you're such a blabbermouth you can't keep anything quiet." Ruth giggled. "Look at today for example." She gave him one of her knowing looks.

"Okay, point taken."

"You should know, guv, DI Greco from Oldston's been trying to find you," Imogen told Calladine. "He said it was in the nature of keeping you informed and that he's got something on the missing girls."

Calladine reached in his pocket for his phone. Greco wouldn't contact his office unless it was important. He tapped in the number and waited. Julian went back to the bar to get a round of drinks and Imogen pulled up another chair and sat down.

"So, what're you keeping back, Ruth?" Imogen asked with a grin. "What little secret have you got lurking in the shadows of your life?"

Ruth laughed. "Nothing. Wish I had, it'd make life more interesting. What about you, Doc?"

"Open book, me. I work; I don't play much — these days. I don't have the energy anymore."

Calladine stood apart from the group and was listening intently to what Stephen Greco was telling him. His face was pulled into a grim frown. He definitely wasn't happy about something.

"They've got something," he told them when he got off the phone. "CCTV has thrown up a van, a large black van present outside both the schools the girls went to."

"So why the face?" Ruth asked.

"They've got a registration, but true to form he doesn't want us involved. I've offered our help but he refused."

"In that case, leave him to it."

"Isla Prideau lived — lives," he corrected himself, "in Leesdon. We should be involved. Greco was only letting me know because he was observing protocol. Bloody good, isn't it?"

The news had utterly flattened him. He picked up the beer Julian had bought for him and downed it fast.

"I'm getting off. Sorry, Doc. That bit of news has really pissed me off. I'd be very poor company if I stayed."

He'd had enough. The day was getting no better. He'd be better off at home alone, sitting in front of his fire. But he wasn't going to get the chance.

"So this is where you're hiding!" The voice was husky.

It almost made him jump it was so unexpected.

"Amy, I . . . I'm sorry," he was floundering. Less than half an hour ago he'd told her he was tired and off home. Now she'd found him in here boozing with his mates. He felt like a naughty school kid again. Whatever he said it would sound like a lie, or a lame excuse. "I was going home, honest, but they dragged me here instead." Yep, feeble, and he could tell by her look that Amy wasn't convinced. But then again she didn't look annoyed either — more, slightly amused.

"These are some of my colleagues," he said hurriedly, hoping the introductions would mask his embarrassment. "You've met Ruth, and this is Imogen and Julian. The sad character with his face in his beer pot is the Doc." He smiled.

"I've not seen you in a while, Jules. Your mum alright, is she?" Amy nodded to the others and addressed these words to Julian.

Julian Batho gave her a broad smile and nodded. So they knew each other. Calladine was taken by surprise. They were a most unlikely pair — Amy the seer and Julian the scientist. How did that work?

"Jules is my nephew," Amy explained. "His mum is my sister, Avril."

"*Jules*," Calladine teased. "Well, you should have said. Now I know how you knew all that stuff about the cards. Why not just come clean? You could have told us. We wouldn't have ribbed you about it. Much."

Amy laughed, unbuttoning her coat and seating herself. "No, you wouldn't or you'd have had me to answer to. But it's not important. So, come on, what are you doing here when you are supposed to be seeing me?" She tugged at his arm and pulled up another chair. "I'll have a gin and tonic please, Jules."

"I was just off when you caught me," admitted Calladine. "It's been one of those days and now I've just had some news that's crowned it good and proper."

"It is their case, boss," Ruth reminded him. "Oldston have the resources, the manpower . . . Don't you think we've got our hands full enough as it is?"

128

Calladine knew Ruth was right but it still galled him. Isla Prideau had been taken from his patch, so it should be down to him to find her.

"I'm terrible company right now, Amy," he apologised. "I won't stay long but you might want to catch up with Julian."

But Julian Batho was over by the door deep in conversation on his mobile phone.

"I came here to find you. But if you really want to go, I could come with you. We could go to yours or mine, I don't mind which."

"I wouldn't be much fun, Amy. I'm done in."

"Is that really how it is? Or have you had enough of me before we even get going?" She was whispering in his ear.

"I'm not spinning you a yarn. I need to sleep. I didn't get home last night, remember?"

"Okay, I understand. We'll get together over the weekend — I'll cook," she whispered again. "But if you cry wolf, Tom Calladine, I'll have to get heavy." And she winked. "You are not getting away from me that easily."

"Will you be okay if I go?"

"Of course. I'm not a baby. Anyway, I want to get to know Julian's new girl a little better. She's one of yours, isn't she?"

"Yep, and Imogen's a bloody good cop so don't go putting the wind up her with all that other stuff."

"Get out of here!" She grinned. "I can see you're going to be something of a project, but I'll make a believer out of you yet."

A quick peck on Amy's cheek, a wave to Doc Hoyle and the others, and he was gone.

* * *

Calladine had to admit he was relieved to get away so easily. Much as he liked Amy, he was in no mood to spend the night with her. Perhaps he was getting old after all. He sighed. It was dark and cold, a perfect night for lazing in front of a warm fire. It took him only minutes to walk to his cottage. As he entered, his phone rang.

It was Zoe.

"Dad! Are you okay? I've been worried sick. It's taken me till now to sort out Lydia, but she's gone now."

"Gone where?"

"She didn't tell me and to be honest, I really don't want to know. That woman is a nightmare at times. She can be so . . . well, so needy. She cried on Jo's shoulder for most of the afternoon then got down and serious on her phone. The upshot was she got a call about an hour ago, which seemed to make her happier, then she took her stuff and left."

"Did she leave any message for me? Did she say anything?"

"I think you were the last thing on her mind. She strikes me as the kind of woman who once she's dealt with the emotional stuff can wipe someone from her life without a backward glance."

"So you reckon I've been wiped, do you?"

"Yes, Dad, I do. And if you ask me you're lucky to be free of her. I know she took care of you when you were injured, but she doesn't half have some edge to her."

"Thanks for dealing with her, Zo. I'm grateful, really."

"Anyway — what you said about your mum — was that the truth or some ploy to spoil Lydia's plans?"

"No — it's true, every last word. I never knew, never even suspected, but Freda must have felt guilty or something because she left me a box of stuff to back everything up."

"Do you know what happened?"

"In a nutshell, my dad had an affair and produced me with another woman. I've never even met her. I know her name from the letter Freda left me but I only found out today who she is."

"So who is she?"

"Zo — for now, I'd rather not say. I won't keep things to myself for much longer but it's complicated and loosely mixed up with a case we're working on at the moment."

"But you will tell me, and I can see what's in the tin sometime, can't I?"

"If you want, Zo. In fact you can keep it for me, if you will? Perhaps I'll bring it round at the weekend. You can have a look, read the letters and make up your own mind about it all."

# CHAPTER 16

Harriet wore the grey wig, a woollen hat and her black coat. She didn't want to be noticed. Walking was becoming more and more difficult, so she also took her stick, the one with the blade hidden inside it. Anyone who saw her would simply see an old lady and pay her no attention. She caught the bus from the end of her avenue and got off at Oldston bus station. From here it was only a five minute walk to the library.

It was closed or she'd have waited inside but there was a small garden with a hedge so she tucked herself in behind it to wait. The occasional passer-by took no notice of her — she was one of the invisible old.

She spotted him as soon as he turned the corner onto the street. Yuri was a thickset man with broad shoulders and a bald head. He wasn't particularly tall and walked with a slight swagger. As he got closer he stopped to light a cigarette and Harriet saw the tattoo on his lower arm — a snake.

She shuffled out and coughed, clutching a hankie to her mouth. She stopped and fumbled in her bag for a second or two. He did not even look. He was waiting for a redhead in the fur coat.

"Excuse me!" she called to him. "Do you have the time? My son was supposed to pick me up but I think he must be running late."

He swore in some foreign tongue and flung the cigarette to the ground. He looked at her briefly and then checked his watch.

"Eight." He barked it out, zipping up his leather jacket against the cold wind.

"I don't know how I'll get home now," she grumbled. "He doesn't usually let me down. He's a good boy."

He cleared his throat and spat onto the ground. He turned his back on her. His girth made him a perfect target. Harriet gave a quick look at the surrounding buildings. She couldn't see any CCTV, but you could never be sure. But even if she was caught on camera, no one would recognise her. There was not a soul on the street.

He was talking to someone on his phone, oblivious of her presence. Harriet pressed the button on the stick, lifted it horizontally, took aim and held her breath. The blade sprang out, bright and sharp. This was going to be good. This man deserved everything that was coming to him. She crept a couple of steps towards him and then lunged with all her strength, spearing him in his lower back. *Like meat on a skewer*, laughed the voice.

He gasped and then gave a low groan. His legs crumpled and he sank to the pavement, where he lay prone. His head had turned to one side, his eyes were open, his arms flailing around wildly. He screamed for help. Harriet stood over him.

"Sick bastard. Not such a hard nut now, are you?" She felt triumphant. The hard nut had been no match for Harriet. She laughed. Who'd have thought it, eh? A sick, dying woman and the tough people trafficker. She aimed a kick at his kidneys and another to the head.

"The only fitting retribution for those children is for you to die. You gave up your right to live the day you started with the children. What do you think of that, Yuri?"

He was silent and his eyes were wide with fright. Harriet knew there must be little fight left in him. She'd had enough too. It was too cold to wait any longer. She placed the blood-stained blade against the side of his neck just above his carotid artery and pushed hard with all her remaining strength. It was over in seconds. One final shudder and Yuri was dead.

It was time to go. Harriet took a card from her coat pocket and stuffed it into his hand. It was the Eight of Swords — one of its meanings was entrapment. Perfect.

\* \* \*

*Friday*

"DS Quickenden has been on from Oldston nick, sir. He says they've found a body. It looks like the victim was killed sometime last night."

Calladine tore his eyes from the incident board and looked at Rocco. "So? What's it got to do with us? They've got DI Supercop to sort it out."

"A tarot card was left at the scene. He thought he'd give me the heads up. It's got them flummoxed." He grinned. "He's also given me the partial registration number for that black van."

"Useful contact this DS."

"Don't be too sure, sir," Imogen butted in. "He's got a reputation for being a bit on the wild side has Jed Quickenden."

"Check the van out would you, Imogen? We'll go from there."

Oldston. Why Oldston? Calladine wondered. Was their killer branching out? "In that case it is one of ours." He reached for the phone and dialled the number for Oldston nick. Seconds later he was speaking to Greco.

"We've had three in the past week. We should talk, compare findings." There was a pause while Calladine listened, pulling a face. "Okay," he said at last. "I'll wait until you get here. Any chance you'll have a preliminary PM report?" He shook his head at the reply. The man was hard work. "He's coming in," he told Rocco. "When he gets here I'll have a short chat with him in my office, to compare what we've got. Then I'll bring the team up to speed."

"What was the card, sir — the one left behind?"

"The Eight of Swords." He gave a shrug. "Means nothing to me."

Calladine disappeared into his office and closed the door behind him. He took his mobile from his jacket pocket and rang Amy.

"Morning, gorgeous! Not a social call I'm afraid. We've had another one and I need your help."

"Ask away, Tom."

"The Eight of Swords. Why would it be left at a murder scene? What's the killer trying to tell us with this one?"

"It could be many things. Generally speaking swords are not good cards. It is possible that he was lured to his death on some pretext and met his end instead."

"Thanks, Amy. I'll see you later with any luck."

It didn't really help. Out in the incident room Calladine poured himself a coffee and pinned the card to the board — it came from Ruth's pack. Their killer was a considerate soul. Without the cards they'd have very little to link the murders together. So why leave them? The doc and he had talked about a list, a bucket list. Could this be the work of someone getting even because of an anniversary, or because they were short of time? Either way the person they were looking for was on a mission and wanted the deaths to be linked.

"Ruth's late," remarked Rocco. "Is she chasing up on something?"

Calladine grunted an unintelligible reply. She'd gone for her first scan. He hoped everything had gone okay. Besides the fact that he didn't want any drama at the moment, Ruth was a good friend, and he wanted her to be happy.

\* \* \*

Twenty minutes or so later, Imogen announced that DI Greco had arrived.

"We'll talk in here." Calladine grabbed the case file and led the way into his office.

Once they were seated Calladine laid out the various reports, photos of the scenes and the cards. Greco had brought only two photos — one of the tarot card, and another of the body.

"Do you have a name for your victim?" Calladine asked.

"No. He had no identification on him, apart from his phone. But that had only been used to make and receive calls from one or two numbers. All pay as you go and currently all turned off."

"How was he killed? Have we got any forensics?"

"He was knifed. The blade pierced one of his kidneys and was long enough to cut through the lower lobe of one lung. The pathologist still has to confirm but a second cut was made to his neck; it cut through his carotid. Forensically there is nothing. It rained last night, threw it down, and he wasn't found until the early hours."

"Still, you can have his DNA profile done. He could be on the database."

"Inspector, the victim's DNA profile is not your concern. He is our body. This is our case."

"But you have to acknowledge that they're linked. They must be. Our first victim was killed with a blade — a long narrow one. We think it might have been concealed in a walking stick. Have you checked CCTV?"

Greco looked at Calladine with a frown on his face. "Look, Inspector — I do know my job. How can you be so sure that the blade had been hidden?"

"A snippet of film we got from a witness," Calladine told him. "What looked like a woman shuffling along the road with a walking stick."

"You don't know for sure though, do you? Your woman may have had nothing to do with the killing." Greco didn't look impressed. "I see from your notes how much is based on assumption. The retribution theory for example. This matching the method of killing to something from the past. It doesn't work, not really, does it? It wouldn't get past a jury."

"It will when we get more meat on the bone. I trust my instincts. They're not just wild theories. I've been a cop for years and I have a reasonable idea how these things work, and how a killer's mind operates. We have a killer; he or she has a list of people they want to get rid of. The method of dispatch they choose is meaningful in some way. We are investigating the death of Albert North and when we find a set of old case notes I will be able to prove it. Don't you work on your hunches, Steve?"

"As I've told you before, it's Stephen."

This was getting boring.

"And no I don't. I gave that up a long time ago. I don't do theories; I do proof, solid evidence. And you should know from the start that I have no plans to hand this over to you."

Calladine watched as Greco's expression hardened. The only sign of humanity in him was a nerve that twitched high on his cheek. Irritation, assumed Calladine.

"I saw the other incident board in the main office — the one for the missing children. That case is currently being dealt with by a team at Oldston, headed by me. It has nothing to do with you. I don't understand what you hope to gain by getting involved."

The man was being a real pain in the arse. It'd been a while since Calladine had met anyone so pedantic.

"What I hope to gain, Inspector, is to get those kids back. And frankly I don't give a toss whose toes I tread on to do it. Isla Prideau went missing from Leesworth — don't forget that. Later today I intend to go and speak to her parents."

"You'll do no such thing. You can't work both cases. You don't have the manpower for a start."

Calladine wanted very much to tell him that he'd do exactly what he bloody liked. But he didn't. He swallowed his expletives and decided on a different tactic.

"We could combine our resources — help each other out. My team are keen to cooperate and share findings on both cases — the murders and the missing kids. So why don't you get off that bloody high horse you seem so fond of?"

Greco was silent, his face frozen. Several seconds passed and neither man spoke.

"Like it or not, the fact is your team is getting nowhere fast. It's been over a week and what have you got? A brief glimpse of a black van," said Calladine.

"Who told you that?"

"Never mind, it's not important. It strikes me that the case needs a bomb up its backside. Don't you feel anything for those girls' families?"

"Of course I feel for them. I have a daughter of my own; she's the same age."

Somehow Calladine couldn't picture Greco as the doting father.

"Have you considered that what happened around here might not be the full extent of the problem? Have you looked at other cases of missing kids? You should take a serious look at what Imogen found. Investigate who has accessed the two mothers' Facebook accounts."

"Inspector, at this very moment there is an entire team looking at exactly that. In fact, if you don't drop this you'll jeopardise a major operation at a crucial point. We know that we are looking at a trafficking ring. Central is up to speed and has invested both time and effort making contact with these people."

Calladine was genuinely surprised. He'd heard nothing about this, but then he'd been out of action for a while. "Contact them? How? You can't just phone them up."

"Through the dark web, Inspector," Greco explained. "Central has gained the confidence of a gang member. A sting is in the process of being set up. The last thing they need is you wading in and ruining months of work."

The dark web? What in hell's name was that? He'd only just got to grips with the surface one and that was dark enough as far as he could see.

"So, you do know your job," he conceded.

"Yes, and you must appreciate, now, that there are things going on that you are not privy to."

"But the kids are still out there and it strikes me that no amount of surfing, dark or not, is bringing them back. I still say you need help."

"Leave it. That's good advice and you should listen to it. If those kids are still alive and still in the country then they will be found."

"Bollocks — not without more input they won't." This was going nowhere.

"And I didn't disregard DC Goode's information either. I acted on it, promptly. It fed into the information the team at Central already has. You are not the only cop who can get things done you know."

There followed another uncomfortable silence until Greco appeared to shake himself and picked up the photo of Tariq Ahmed. "But perhaps you have a point about the killings. I'll get forensics to see if they can ascertain whether the same weapon was used in both."

It was something at least. "And the kids?"

"That's down to me, my team and Central. So leave it."

* * *

Friday dawned bright and sunny. It was cold, but without the bone-numbing, damp winter gloom there'd been for the last day or so. Harriet Finch was feeling slightly better. Her task was nearly complete. Now she'd dealt with Lessing it was all over and all the names on her list had been crossed off. After Lessing, she now had to face the tidying up. She'd go round to his place later, perhaps after dark, and make sure he was suffering as she'd planned. If not — then it was simple. She'd inflict further injuries.

In the good weather she decided to tidy up her back garden, and get some fresh air into the bargain. The autumn leaves had lain sodden on the garden path for long enough.

She hummed to herself as she worked. Uppermost on her mind was what to do about Lessing's phone. She'd wait until later, after she'd heard the news. If the news didn't mention anything about finding him, and his involvement with the children's kidnap, then she'd have to get it to the police. Harriet decided to work on the detail later.

She did her work a little at a time, brushing the leaves into piles to be shovelled up later if she felt up to it. Harriet was so lost in her own thoughts that she didn't hear the back gate open, nor did she hear the footsteps until it was too late.

"Want some help?" Harriet spun round. He was young, tall and wiry looking. He was wearing those jeans that bagged and hung loose around the rear end. He looked shifty and she felt suddenly afraid, which wasn't like her at all. This was followed by an almost uncontrollable urge to laugh out loud. What was this? She was scared of nothing, not any more. She was a cold-hearted killer for heaven's sake! So what was it about this lad that scared her?

"I'll finish up here for a tenner — what d'you say? You could go and brew up, I fancy a cuppa." He grinned, rubbing his hands together.

"Who are you? You've no right to come in here uninvited." Harriet waved him back the way he'd come. "Go on! Get out before I call the police and have you dragged off."

He was tutting — *tutting!* The cheek of him! "I mean it." She pulled off her gardening gloves and threw them to the ground.

"It was an offer of help. But seeing that you don't want to play the game then I'll have to do this the hard way."

What did he mean, *the hard way?*

"Remember the old man? The one sat on that bench on the common, the one called Albert North," he said moving a couple of steps closer to her. "Helpless he was, helpless and ill. He couldn't fight back and he wouldn't harm a fly. Remember him now?"

"Of course I remember him; I'm not senile. Friend of yours was he?"

"My uncle, that's who he was. And you killed him — murdering cow!"

His eyes were set too close together — he could well be one of the North clan, wicked lot all of them. "Setting fire to that villain was one of the most satisfying things I've ever done," she told him.

She could see no sense in denying it, and anyway, he'd already shown his hand. He'd obviously come here to exact some sort of retribution — which was rich, given what North had done to her son.

"What do you expect me to do, young man? The bastard's dead!"

"And you killed him. You set him alight and left him to suffer. You're a cruel, vicious bitch, and now you're going to get yours."

He meant it. There was real hatred in his young eyes. It fascinated her because she understood it so well. He stepped closer and she saw he was clutching a baseball bat in his hand. Why hadn't she spotted that before? How very remiss of her; she was slipping, must be the medication.

"What do you imagine will happen if you strike me with that?"

She smiled; it was obvious that her words had surprised him. He scowled at her, and lowered the bat.

"Whatever, it'll be worth it to see you suffer like he did. I'll get you across the legs first — break 'em both and send you to the ground. Then I'll do your head."

He had all the right words. They sounded a lot like those she'd used herself recently. Harriet nodded. It was a good plan. In different circumstances she could have warmed to this young man.

"My neighbour is watching us, right now, from his kitchen window." She looked towards it and waved a casual greeting. "One shout, one scream and he'll be here in a flash. Also there are probably another dozen or so pairs of eyes on you as we speak. Haven't you noticed the block of flats behind you? All those windows overlooking my garden? Still fancy your chances?"

"Shut up, bitch!" He looked around anxiously. He didn't want to be seen — he was well known, easily recognised. "Get in that shed — go on, get in now."

Harriet sighed, turned and walked towards her large garden shed. When he'd been alive her husband had used it as a workshop. Not only was it large but it was well equipped too. She wasn't worried now, her earlier panic had subsided. She'd just have to deal with him: another name to add to the list.

"Nice." Jayden North looked around at the workbench and the tools so neatly arranged.

"My husband could turn his hand to anything," Harriet told him proudly. "He did up the entire house after he retired. He made all my kitchen units."

"Why? Why did you do that to Uncle Albert?" He moved towards her.

"Because he killed my son. There — a simple explanation and one that should suffice even for an idiot like you."

"I'm not an idiot."

"Yes you are. You're an uneducated idiot with a background completely lacking in any sort of adult guidance. North was a brute, a drunken lout without any morals at all. You must know that. He killed anyone that got in his way, and not just my son either. Over the years he dispatched any number of the rogues and villains who crossed him — innocent people too. The world should be grateful to me."

It worked. Jayden North lost control and lunged forward at her with the bat held high. But before he could strike, Harriet dodged to the side, sticking out her foot to trip him up. He tumbled headlong onto the bench. He was bent at the waist, his hands sprawled forwards, face red with anger, and winded by the force of his landing. The bat rolled away across the floor out of his reach.

Perfect. Harriet took the cordless drill from its holder on the wall and held it to Jayden North's face like a revolver.

"Not so full of accusations now, are you lad?"

She fired the drill, making it buzz centimetres from his left ear.

"How much damage do you reckon I could do with this?"

Jayden recovered his breath. "I'll bloody do for you — stupid old bitch!"

He made to raise himself up but Harriet was too quick for him. She lowered the drill bit from his ear to his neck and pressing the tip on his carotid artery she squeezed the *on* switch with her forefinger.

The bit went in so smoothly it surprised her. Jayden North blinked once and slithered to the floor in shock from the sudden catastrophic blood loss. It spurted in a thick red torrent, covering everything, and Harriet moved away in disgust. Remarkably, she didn't like blood; she was squeamish. She watched from a distance as his body twitched and shook. His eyes, full of bewilderment, searched her face, as the blood pumped relentlessly from his neck. One last jerk, his face contorted, and he moved no more. It had taken only seconds; he wouldn't have suffered much, she reasoned. But now that it was over, she had another body on her hands.

Harriet stepped over his still frame and replaced the drill on its hanger. She took an old tarpaulin that lay folded in a corner and pulled it over him. It was large enough to cover both Jayden North and the blood which was now spread all around him. Should anyone casually look in, they'd see nothing. Job done.

Harriet locked the shed door behind her and dropped the key down the grid on the path. The incident had given Harriet new strength and with her frail health, this wasn't something to be squandered. Now was the time to make that final check on Lessing before exhaustion set in, as it inevitably would.

# CHAPTER 17

Once Greco had left, Calladine called a case team meeting. He wanted to bring together all their findings. Maybe someone would have a bright idea. By the time they were all assembled he'd already been on the phone to see if Doc Hoyle had remembered anything about the post-mortem he'd worked on years ago — the one involving fire — but he hadn't. They badly needed a break.

"It looks highly likely that the killing in Oldston last night was done by our man. Or woman," he added. "This victim is something of a puzzle. He had no identity on him for a start. His phone was used only for a couple of numbers — why? What are we looking at?"

"A drug dealer?" Rocco suggested. "They tend to have a dedicated phone."

"For all their deals though, not just for a couple," corrected Imogen.

"Give it some thought. It might lead somewhere."

At that moment Ruth joined them. Calladine looked up and smiled; she was looking decidedly perky.

"Okay?"

"Just perfect," she replied. "Can I say something, sir?" Calladine stood aside and waved her to the front of the room.

"I've got some news," she said to the three of them. "We've spoken to family already so you lot are next on the list." She paused and looked round at Calladine. "Jake and I are having a baby. I'm late for work because we've been for the first scan."

Calladine smiled as the team gave a huge cheer and Rocco whistled. Imogen rushed over to give her a hug.

"It's great news!" he said.

"Do you have a piccy?" asked Imogen.

"Yes, here." And she passed her the image.

"Do you know what it is?" asked Calladine.

"Don't be daft — it's far too early. Perhaps next time."

Calladine looked at the grainy black-and-white picture and, try as he might, he couldn't see a baby.

"Have I missed much?"

"A visit from DI Greco," Calladine said, pulling a face, "that and another body in Oldston. And it's one of ours — a tarot card was left at the scene."

"Do we have a name?"

"We have nothing. Greco is reluctant to share. But in any event there was no ID on him, only a phone."

\* \* \*

Harriet let herself into Lessing's house. The place was cold and still. As she stood in the hallway she couldn't hear a sound, not even a whimper. He was either dead or unconscious.

She made her way carefully down the stone staircase to the cellar where she'd left him to rot. The first thing that struck her was the smell of damp. A sickly, cloying coldness mixed with mould made her wrinkle her nose and cover her mouth with her hand.

"Gordon!" she called out. "Can you hear me?"

She could see him lying in the middle of the stone floor where she'd left him. For several seconds he was still, but then he twitched. He must have the constitution of an ox! He'd heard her and was moving his tied hands feebly in the air above him.

This was Harriet's opportunity to ask him about the children. She strode towards the crumpled heap and yanked the scarf from his face.

"Where have you taken them, Gordon, the two little girls?"

His legs were bleeding and from the way they were lying, it was obvious they were broken.

"Harriet," he whispered. "Help . . . me, please, for pity's sake . . ."

"No — not until you tell me what you've done with them."

He moaned again and shut his eyes.

"They're gone. You can't help them but you can help me . . ."

Harriet delivered a sharp kick to his right calf and he shrieked in agony. "You're a bastard, a cruel wicked bastard, Gordon Lessing. You'll get no help from me until you tell me. I know you find them and that Yuri takes them. Yuri's dead now. So don't get any ideas that he'll come and help you."

She kicked him again, and this time he didn't even have the strength to scream. She felt nothing — no remorse, no pity. Why was that? This wasn't who she was!

*Because you hate him, because where he's concerned, you're beyond pity.*

"Show me some mercy — please," he groaned. "I was married to your sister . . ." He surprised her then by weeping, the tears running in dirty streaks down his fat face. "Loosen my hands . . . please, please . . . help me. I'm in agony. You can't imagine the pain."

"That's where you're wrong, Gordon. I can imagine it very well. I have terminal cancer, remember? You'll get nothing from me until I find those children. And what about Sybil? You killed her, you scum. You showed Sybil no mercy at all. My poor sister died in agony because of what you did. You left her alone, injured, to die of cold. So tell me Gordon, why should I help you?"

"If I die then so will those girls." A hard edge crept into his voice. "Without me, they'll never be found. Think of that, Harriet. It's not just me you're condemning to a long, painful death. You will have their blood on your hands too because you could have saved them."

Harriet was torn. She wanted to help the children, of course she did; none of this had anything to do with them. "I want you to die like she did. I want you to suffer like Sybil. There is no help, no one is coming, so you might as well give up and tell me what you know."

"Free me first — get me some help — an ambulance — then I'll tell you."

Harriet didn't trust him. Despite his injuries, if she freed him she was risking her own safety. If she got him some help he still might not talk — why should he? He'd be incriminating himself in a dreadful crime. She had to think.

"By now the police will know all about Yuri." That was what she hoped anyway. "They'll work things out, they have experts."

"You can't be sure though, can you? Yuri's a shadow, he doesn't exist. The police won't get anywhere."

A shadow — an illegal immigrant, she surmised. He'd be lying in the morgue: this week's big mystery. She heard Lessing groan. He wasn't going to help her. She gave him another sharp kick and he lost consciousness again.

Harriet looked around in the gloom of the cellar. She needed something . . . she had to make this end but not too quickly. She wouldn't be coming here again; she was too ill. It was time for him to go for good. He was bleeding and in pain but if by chance someone came down here, a cleaner or even Jane then he might still be found.

She had her stick with her. This wasn't how she'd wanted him to die, but there was no choice. Exposing the blade, Harriet placed it over where she thought his heart would be. "Goodbye, Gordon," she said to the unconscious man. "You are lucky, this will be quick and it's more than you deserve."

One long, steady push and the blade slid into his flesh. It went in between two ribs and he was dead in seconds. His shameful life was finally done with.

There was just one job left to do. Harriet took the card from her pocket and placed it on a dry patch of floor at the back of Lessing's head. The Ten of Swords. The meaning was unmistakable. The card depicted multiple swords piercing a bleeding heart.

First Jayden North and now Lessing. It had been a busy morning and Harriet was exhausted — exhausted and very ill. The pain was getting worse. Deep in the very centre of her body, the pain radiated out to every inch of her frail form and she was beginning to feel as if she was being slowly crucified. She knew that very soon the cancer would suck the life from her and she'd be gone. It was time to stop for now; she must rest.

Harriet dragged her weary body back to the car. Before she went home she'd stop off at Nesta's house and give her the tickets. The exhibition was today — Nesta's birthday.

It had all been too much for her, all her strength was gone but the problem of what to do about the children wouldn't let her rest. Harriet went home and put herself to bed, but sleep eluded her.

She had to get Lessing's phone to the police. She was no expert; all she could see were texts and photos but the police had people who'd know how to examine it properly. How to do it?

Harriet couldn't take it into the police station herself because of the cameras. Posting the thing would take too long, and it might lie in a pile of unopened mail for several days, days that the little girls didn't have.

The best bet was to leave it somewhere safe and call the police anonymously. She'd make it clear that the phone was valuable evidence in the missing children case — they wouldn't ignore that, surely?

Harriet took her medication and drifted off to sleep. When she woke up, it was early afternoon. The sleep had done her good, but better than that, she had a plan.

She'd go to the supermarket, the large one off the bypass. She'd call the police from Lessing's mobile and then leave it in a trolley locked in one of those booths where you can leave your shopping while you eat in the café.

Perfect. All she had to do was ensure that the cameras didn't catch her. But did it really matter if they did? Even if she was caught red-handed what could the law do to her? All along, that had been the beauty of her plan. Her illness — terminal — granted her impunity. Harriet's spirits rose.

\* \* \*

Since today was a Friday the supermarket was extra busy — and full of stupid people. They got in her way with their kids and their insistence on stopping mid-aisle to chat. Harriet cursed audibly to herself as she negotiated the gossiping shoppers and picked a few items from the shelves. She bought cheap stuff. She was going to have to pay for these, but she wouldn't be taking them home.

She wore a hat with a brim that she'd pulled down over her forehead. That and her coat collar turned up would hide her face from the cameras. But Harriet was also aware that she must be running out of time. Her luck had to run out at some stage, surely? She'd miss it — the excitement, the planning and, most of all, the climax of the murder itself. It was so addictive, and part of her never wanted it to end.

When she had a few items in the trolley she made for a quiet corner of the store. The area displaying kitchen goods was mostly empty, and she didn't want to be overheard. Harriet took the phone from her pocket and tapped in the number for Oldston Police Station. She'd thought about this carefully and chosen Oldston rather than Leesdon because she'd read that it was Oldston which was handling the missing girls case.

"Don't speak. Just listen," she growled when someone answered. "A phone, in a trolley in booth twelve at the Leesdon

Supermarket — there's information there that will help you find the girls."

There. She'd told them. The police had what they needed now. It shouldn't take them long to find it. Harriet headed over to park her trolley. She placed the phone under a loaf of bread, pushed the trolley into booth twelve, locked the door and made for the exit. She decided to go home and listen to the local news on the radio. It was done.

# CHAPTER 18

"Inspector!" Julian called out as Calladine entered the incident room. "Sorry to disturb but I think you'll want to hear this."

The forensic scientist approached Calladine with a smile on his face. He obviously had something positive to tell them.

"Some news you will undoubtedly find interesting."

Calladine looked up at him — he was actually grinning, and that didn't often happen with Julian.

"There's been a tip-off. I'm not sure how involved you are with the missing children case but Oldston police received a call about half an hour ago. The caller told them to go to the supermarket — the one off the bypass — and they'd find a phone."

"DI Greco will have your balls for this." Calladine raised his eyebrows. "He was here today and he made it quite plain whose case it was."

"That's as may be, but this does concern you. Oldston outsource all their forensics; they use a provider, the Duggan Centre on the outskirts of Manchester. An old university pal from there has just given me the heads up that DNA found on the phone matches a trace on the tarot card found with the unidentified body in Oldston."

"Could the dead man have touched the card?"

"He could have," Julian agreed. "But the DNA is also a match for what we've collected — from the hair, the beaker and the other cards. There is no mistake."

Calladine was more than surprised. The murders and the missing kids — linked?

"Are you sure, Julian? There's no chance of cross-contamination?"

"Certainly not, Inspector. The phone was never in my lab."

"And you're positive it belonged to someone involved with the disappearances?"

"Yes, Inspector. It was used to call only a very few numbers — one of them is that of a known trafficker who vice have been watching for some time."

So their killer had a hand in taking the kids. But that didn't sound like a person on a mission of vengeance. He looked around at the others; they were silent, thoughtful. The same questions were obviously filling their heads.

"But we still don't have a match on the database — not for your killer or the other DNA evidence we found."

"Anyone got any ideas?" His own mind was racing.

"I've had to give this information to DI Greco; he is the SIO — so you'll be hearing all this from him too."

"I doubt that, Julian. DI Greco doesn't like to share. But thanks for the information. When I figure out what to do with it we might get somewhere."

"I've compiled this." Julian offered him a sheet of A4. "It's a list of calls made and received from the supermarket phone. Greco's lot have already checked and the phone is a "pay as you go." It's never been registered so he's no idea who it belonged to. But they do need topping up . . ." He winked.

"And the dead man's phone was used to call the phone found in the supermarket?"

Julian nodded.

"Thanks. We owe you — at least it's something."

When Julian had left, he turned to his team. "We also have the ticket numbers, remember? That art exhibition is today at the community centre. Rocco, get a uniform to check the guests. If they are presented I want to know at once."

"Julian's right, those phones do need topping up," Imogen offered. "I'll check and see if the owner ever paid for one with a debit or credit card. Very often people buy credit when they're doing the weekly shop."

"They wouldn't be so careless, surely?"

"It's something to try." Imogen shrugged.

She had a point. Calladine watched as the DC got up and made for her desk. Extracting this sort of information was Imogen's forte. "You do realise that DI Greco will be making exactly the same checks, don't you?" Ruth reminded him. "He's a good cop and he'll be on it right away."

"So what are you saying? That we should give up, hand the lot over to him and go put our feet up?"

"No, of course not, but if the two of you got your heads together and came to some agreement, the case might be solved a lot sooner."

"No, it wouldn't. It'll end with our team doing all the legwork and Greco making the arrest we've worked for. So for now we'll leave DI bloody Greco to work things out for himself."

"It'll end badly, you know. You'll end up rowing, either with Greco or with Long, because once our acting DCI gets wind of this he'll be on at you to cooperate."

"And I will," Calladine allowed coolly. "But in my own way, and not until I'm ready. But for now, until Imogen comes up with something, we go over everything we've got — every last detail — and we keep the tickets thing under wraps."

"Does Long know about the tickets?"

"I gave him a very short report the other day, Ruth. If he deigned to read it then yes, he does."

"Then he could have given that information to Greco already."

"I don't think so, because if he had, the brilliant detective would be in our faces as we speak."

"Sir!" a triumphant Imogen called out. "He did top up with his debit card. Two weeks ago at a supermarket in Oldston. I've got his name and address — he's local too."

Just the break they needed.

"Check if he's got form, Imogen, anything — even a parking ticket."

"No, sir, there's nothing on him," she confirmed within minutes. "But he does own a black van and that partial number we've got fits."

Bingo!

It appeared that Gordon Lessing had only once paid for a mobile phone top-up using his card. But that was all it had taken to identify him. Calladine decided that both Ruth and Imogen should go with him to the address. The young DC deserved to be in on the collar. She'd had the bright idea in the first place and then found the information in record time.

"Where locally?"

"Those houses along Thunder Lane."

"Expensive."

"Yes, but we've a shrewd idea how he made his money now, haven't we, sir?" was Ruth's comment. "People like that deserve all that's coming to them. I hope the bastard rots in hell."

Calladine shot her a look. The case was getting to her which was rare. It involved missing children. She was pregnant, emotional — perhaps she should stay here.

"Stake out the community centre if you want, Ruth — me and Imogen can do this," he suggested.

"No way. I know what you're thinking, Tom, but you're wrong. I have a job to do and that's what's going to happen."

* * *

They went in Calladine's car. No one said much on the short journey to Thunder Lane. Calladine was lost in his thoughts and Ruth was keeping her own counsel.

"Looks like you were right, sir, reeks of money round here," Imogen remarked as they pulled up outside the imposing property. "These go for a small fortune I'll bet."

"How do we play it?" Ruth asked.

"I think we'll knock on the front door, Ruth with me. Imogen, make your way around that path and watch the back."

"I just hope he doesn't produce any sort of weapon, sir. We're hardly mob-handed, are we?"

"You okay with this?" He nodded at Ruth's belly. "Perhaps you would have been better keeping an eye on the exhibition after all."

"Don't you even try, Tom," she warned him. "I'm perfectly fit and up to the job. Trust me, I'll let you know when I'm not, and keep your voice down. Imogen's only feet away and I don't want the team thinking I've turned into some sort of softie overnight."

Seemed he couldn't do anything right.

The two detectives made their way to the front door and rang the bell. The curtains were open in the downstairs windows and everything looked neat and tidy inside. But there was no answer. Ruth went to the garage and peered through the window. A large saloon car was parked inside, so if Lessing was out then he was on foot.

"Sir!" Imogen called. "The back door's open."

"How very fortuitous." Calladine smiled. "Come on then, let's take a look."

"It's all very quiet, sir, and there's a funny smell," Imogen said, holding her nose.

"Vile smell, you mean," Ruth corrected. "Smells like damp, Imogen, damp and vomit."

"Vomit?"

"Well, vomit and other bodily functions," Ruth explained as politely as she could. "Seems to me that someone's had a bad night."

"Mr Lessing!" Calladine called out. "Anyone in?"

They did a quick check of the house but there was no sign of anybody. The heating was off and the place was like ice.

"There's a cellar!" Imogen announced, as she found the door leading from the kitchen. She wrinkled up her nose again. "It's definitely coming from down there, whatever it is."

Calladine went first. "Watch the steps; they're steep and slippery."

It was dark, and for several seconds none of them could see anything. The foul smell was everywhere. It was making Calladine nauseous, and he guessed the others must feel the same. When his eyes had become accustomed to the gloom, Calladine could just make out a shape on the floor.

"Get an ambulance!" Calladine instructed Ruth. This was going to be bad.

Imogen bent down and felt for a pulse in the neck. "I think he's had it, sir. He's bleeding from his chest and frozen. Look at his legs — they look broken. Could he have fallen down those steps and been stuck here all night?"

"I don't think so," Calladine told her. "The stairs are too far away and his hands are cable tied — look. He's been injured and left here to rot. This was no accident."

"He could have crossed one of the traffickers. This could be their way of getting even."

It was a reasonable explanation. In any other circumstances she would have been right — but not this time.

"I don't think so, Imogen." Calladine had spotted the card — the tarot card left on the floor a few inches from the man's head. "That makes it the work of our killer, not some trafficker hell-bent on revenge."

"Ambulance is on its way and I've rung Julian and the doc. They'll be here as soon as."

"Look familiar?"

Ruth met his gaze. She was as puzzled as he was.

"I don't get it — what has this to do with the missing girls?"

"Well, there's a link somewhere. The phone had a known number on it — the number of an Eastern European man that Central has in their sights. In fact it was used to ring and receive calls from that number on many occasions. So, like it or not, there is a link."

"Inspector Calladine!" Stephen Greco made his way down the stairs. "Ours I think," he said, nodding at the body.

"Ordinarily I might agree with you but I'm afraid there are . . . complications." Calladine grinned at his rival.

"No. This one is definitely ours," Greco replied, the warning in his tone clear enough.

"See that?" Calladine pointed to the card. "One of those has been left at each of the murder sites in the current case we're investigating — so this one is *ours*, DI Greco."

Calladine watched DI Greco's face contort in an angry frown, then he spun on his heel and retraced his way up the cellar steps.

"He's not gone far," Ruth assured him. "Long will back him, and you'll get your knuckles rapped yet again." She sighed. "You are your own worst enemy, Tom Calladine, and you just don't learn. Accept that Greco has a part to play and let him in."

"No — and don't tell him anything about our case either."

"I won't need to — it's all on the database."

"I want to know about that card." He wrote the words *Ten of Swords* in his notebook.

"You want an excuse to swan off and see Amy, you mean."

"Stay here with Imogen. Guard this crime scene until Julian and the doc get here."

"Guard it against who, sir? A DI who's senior to me and has every right to know as much we do?"

"Do whatever you think fit." Even he knew that his behaviour was way out of line.

* * *

Ruth had had enough. Calladine's attitude was that of a schoolboy. So DI bloody Greco got on his nerves. Everyone had to work with a pain in the arse occasionally.

"I hope for all our sakes that Stephen Greco doesn't become our new DCI," she told Imogen. "Can you imagine what life would be like with those two constantly sniping?"

"The problem is — he's good. There's no denying it, he's a breath of fresh air. Jones was incompetent, Long's too fond of doing nothing, and, in my opinion, DI Greco would be great."

"Go and discuss that with the boss . . . Anyway, what do you reckon happened to him?" She looked at the body.

There was no doubt in Ruth's mind that Gordon Lessing had been left here to die. This killing was like the others — it satisfied some grudge held by the murderer. What it had to do with the missing girls she couldn't even guess at.

"Whatever happened we'll soon know — the doc's here now!" Imogen called.

Ruth heard his voice as he climbed down the stairs. And he had DI Greco in tow.

"I want the PM report doing promptly and no short cuts," Ruth heard him tell the doc.

She shook her head. The doc wouldn't appreciate being spoken to like that. Having Greco at Leesdon would make working there impossible. He'd have everyone's back up within the first week.

"We do a thorough job but it takes what it takes," the doc replied sharply. It brought a smile to Ruth's face, and so did the look that warned Greco not to tell him how to do his job.

"So, is this the killings or the kidnappings?"

"Both," Ruth interrupted, "although we don't see the tie-up, not yet anyway."

"Is DI Calladine here?" asked the doc.

"No. He's gone off to get some more information about the card that was left. The actual card is over there."

"He's wasting his time." Greco turned to the doc. "Have you asked Doctor Batho to attend?" The doc nodded.

"Then I'm afraid you're wasting his time too. This is my case now, whatever DI Calladine might think. I want this cellar and the rest of the house gone over with a fine tooth comb forensically."

"Julian is always meticulous," Ruth pointed out.

"We outsource our forensic needs at Oldston. Everything we've gleaned from the missing children case is with the Duggan Centre. I would like whatever CSI find here to be sent there too."

Ruth folded her arms. "So you don't need Julian on this? Are you sure? Like I said, he's very good and he gets results."

"I don't doubt it, sergeant, but this is my case so we'll do things my way."

"Poor Julian," she whispered to Imogen.

"I heard that, sergeant." Greco turned round to face both women, grim-faced. "A word to the wise — I know he's very friendly with your team but you should tell him to look to his future, and I doubt it's with the forensic lab at Leesdon General." He indicated the body. "It's this man's phone we recovered in the supermarket, so this is most likely *Gail*," Greco told them.

"The stalker from Facebook," added Imogen.

"Yes, you did well there, working that one out."

He gave praise but without smiling, Ruth noticed.

"Why would these people use someone like Lessing to do their dirty work? He's got no previous — how would they have recruited him?"

"Recruitment — I've no idea, but they'll have used him for exactly that reason — no previous. He was a clean skin — someone not known to the police."

* * *

"He's going to be a problem," Ruth stated, once Greco had left the cellar. "If he gets the DCI post at Leesdon things will never be the same. I doubt we'll ever use Julian and his team again, and goodness knows what else he'd change."

"Well, I think DI Stephen Greco's rather dishy," Imogen said with a smile on her face.

"Don't let Julian hear you say that," Ruth warned.

"Don't let me hear what?" he asked, coming down the steps.

"Over here!" Ruth called to him.

"You should be suited up, the both of you," he said and handed them each a paper coverall.

"Apparently you're not needed," Ruth told him. "All the stuff CSI collect is to be sent to the Duggan Centre."

Ruth watched Julian's face harden. "Am I in or out?" he asked bluntly.

"It's got nothing to do with me or Calladine," Ruth reassured him, holding her hands up. "It's him: Greco. He's a new broom at Oldston nick and out to make his mark."

She rubbed his arm. "Sorry, Julian, but it isn't my call."

# CHAPTER 19

There were one or two customers milling around Amy's shop, mostly interested in the jewellery.

"Tom! Something's up; you look dreadful."

"I need your help again," he said, ignoring the comment and pulling his notebook from his coat pocket. "The Ten of Swords?"

"What of it?"

"What does it mean? It's been left at the scene of another murder." He spoke in a whisper, so the customers wouldn't overhear.

"Well, like the Eight of Swords it's one of the Minor Arcana. You see the Tarot is divided into two halves — the Major and Minor Arcana."

"So our killer is knowledgeable?"

She shrugged. "They could have read a book, looked it up. But back to the card, if it was left at the scene of a killing it suggests someone with a grudge. It signifies that the victim had it coming. It indicates someone with a burning hatred for your victim. When they finally get the opportunity, they stab, stab and stab in a fury — you get the picture." She showed him the graphic image on the card. "It's frenzy. Overkill. It's a bad card, Tom."

161

It certainly had been for Gordon Lessing.

"What are you doing later, say, early evening?" he asked.

"Nothing, but you look as if you have something in mind," she replied, blue eyes sparkling.

"I was thinking of the art exhibition at the community centre — fancy coming?"

"Why? Do you intend to buy something, Tom?"

"No — it's work, but I want to look like one of the punters. You like art anyway, I've seen your flat," he smiled.

"So you want me as part of your cover. How flattering." The blue eyes no longer held a sparkle.

"Well, no, but I don't want to wander around looking like a policeman."

"Okay I'll come, as long as you make it up to me. We could come back here afterwards — have a bite to eat and go from there."

Calladine nodded. After the day he was having, it sounded like a plan.

"We'll walk there. They have wine at those events and I fancy getting you squiffy," Calladine said.

"Squiffy, eh? So you can have your wicked way with me."

He leant forward and kissed her cheek — and then he was gone.

* * *

Calladine went back to the nick. He wanted to know more about Gordon Lessing. Imogen was still at the scene with Ruth so he pounced on Rocco.

"Lessing is dead. Same as the others — well, not exactly the same method, but a card was left. See what we've got on the guy. He's mixed up with the kidnapping of the two girls somewhere along the line, so I can't believe we've got nothing on him."

Rocco spent several minutes checking the police files and then looked up, shaking his head. "There's nothing, sir, not even a motoring offence. The guy's clean."

"How does he earn a living? Get me his bank details. What family has he got? Get me the basics, Rocco. I need something on him and quick."

Greco would be digging up exactly the same stuff. Damn the man! He'd no idea why he'd taken against him so strongly, but he had. The idea that he would probably have to hand the entire case over to Oldston was getting to him. He needed to crack this — and soon.

"Sir! There's been a call from the community centre," Joyce said, popping her head around the office door. "The PC on the door says the tickets you are interested in have been presented, and he's got a couple waiting to see you."

This could be it. Calladine grabbed his coat and made for the stairs. "Rocco — keep on with Lessing. I'll ring you within the hour." He'd ring Ruth too, when he got there, and tell her to join him.

He drove down Leesdon High Street and turned into the community centre car park. The plain-clothes officer who'd been checking the tickets had Nesta and Charlie Dunlop waiting in the office. They were an unremarkable, middle-aged couple. Calladine wasn't sure what he'd been expecting but these two looked very unlike a pair of murderers.

"DI Calladine, Leesworth Police." He flashed his ID. "The tickets for this afternoon, where did you get them?"

"Why? Why's it so important?" Nesta challenged hotly. "It's my birthday. I'm supposed to be having a good time, not sitting in here with him . . ." she nodded at the PC, ". . . like some criminal."

Calladine could see that Nesta Dunlop was clearly annoyed. She was sitting with her handbag on her lap, her face sporting a look that could curdle milk.

"I'm sure we can clear this up," Calladine reassured her. "The tickets are important evidence in a case we're working on."

"D'you hear that, Charlie? Tickets with excitement built in." Now she was smiling. "Harriet doesn't do anything by halves, does she?"

"Harriet?"

"Yes, Inspector, Harriet Finch, my best friend. She gave me those tickets for my birthday. She knows I like things like this. She's so thoughtful."

At last a name — something he could really use.

"Where does she live, this Harriet Finch?"

"Clover Close, number four, just round by the tower block on the estate."

Right under their noses.

"Thank you, Mrs Dunlop. You've been a great help. I hope you enjoy the rest of your day."

Calladine told the PC to keep the couple there long enough for him to reach Harriet Finch, and not to let them make any calls.

\* \* \*

Outside, he sat in his car and rang Ruth.

"We've got a lead, a big one — a name and address for the woman who most likely took the tickets. Harriet Finch, Clover Close — it's a small cul-de-sac off Circle Road. I'll meet you there." He gave her no chance to respond. If she was still at Lessing's house, and Greco was within earshot, Calladine didn't want him getting wind of this.

\* \* \*

"I think you upset DI Greco, sir. He wasn't happy about you being at the scene, and now he's changed all the procedures. It's a case of goodbye Julian and hello the Duggan Centre."

"Hope you didn't tell him anything about what we've got."

Ruth shook her head. "It was hard not to, though. He has every right to know."

"So what did you say?"

"I waffled. Fortunately he was more interested in organising the house search, so I managed to escape."

164

"I'll deal with him later," Calladine assured her. "By the end of the day I'm hoping to have a lot more. I'm sure DI Greco would like as full a picture as we can give him, and we might have something here."

"This isn't like you. Where's your professionalism gone? Sharing information isn't something you usually shy away from."

"We've done all the donkey work. This is our case. Given half a chance he'll swan in and steal the bone from under our noses. Well, that's not happening."

"You're wrong. This attitude you've developed all of a sudden will backfire. But you're not going to listen, are you?"

"He needs to stay in Oldston where he belongs, and then we'll get along just fine."

"Number four — there. Looks okay, neat and clean."

"What do you expect the lair of a serial killer to look like?"

"Well, it's not a flat in a tower block on the Hobfield, is it? It looks ordinary, no sign of grinding poverty, no blaring music or teenagers lurking about. She's even got net curtains."

Calladine knocked on the front door, but there was no answer. Ruth peered through the front window, trying to see through the lacy fabric of the nets.

"She could be out."

"No. She's in. I'm going round the back."

"Be careful. She might be neat and tidy, but she's probably our killer, remember?"

Calladine opened the small gate and wandered round to the back door. It was open.

"Mrs Finch!" He stuck his head through the doorway. "Are you in?"

Ruth suddenly dashed past him. He saw her snatch a pan of boiling potatoes from the hob. It had boiled dry and was about to burn.

"That was careless. You don't think she's got wind and done a runner, do you, guv?"

But Harriet Finch hadn't gone anywhere. She lay shivering on her sitting room carpet. Her face was deathly pale and she was mumbling incoherently. Something was very wrong. This wasn't what the detective had expected to find.

"Get an ambulance," Calladine told Ruth, "and some water."

"Did she fall?" Ruth asked as she tapped in the number.

"I don't think so. I think she's ill." Calladine could see how thin she was and the sparseness of her hair. "Mrs Finch — Harriet." He spoke gently, raising her head a little. "What's happened? Are you not feeling well?"

Her eyes fluttered open and she stared at him for a few moments. "You're police," she whispered. "You've finally worked it out and come for me." And then she smiled.

"DI Calladine and DS Bayliss from Leesdon," he said. "I wanted a word with you about the tickets you gave your friend, Nesta Dunlop."

Harriet looked at him, her gaze steadier now. "I hope she's enjoying herself. I knew she'd like the exhibition . . . I took them from the doctor. You know, I killed him. You should also know that I did North too, and that monster of a brother-in-law of mine, Gordon Lessing."

Calladine nodded to Ruth who had a glass of water in her hand. "You're not well; you might want to wait until you have legal representation."

"There won't be time for any of that. I'm dying, and it won't be long now. My notes are on the sideboard. Over there."

Ruth passed Calladine the thick medical file — it had the word *Terminal* written across the cover. He took it and shuddered — how did a person cope with news like that? He flicked through a few sheets and shook his head.

"Cancer, Ruth. Advanced." He spoke in a whisper. "She was under Doctor Ahmed."

It came as no surprise.

"The man had no soul," Harriet complained. "He was so cold, so matter of fact. I walked out of his clinic on my own that day and broke my heart. He had to go. He had to be the first."

"North?" asked Calladine.

Harriet looked up at the inspector. "He killed my son, Jimmy. He had him beaten and burnt, and all because of a few pounds worth of drugs."

Ruth bent down and put the glass to her lips. "We should record this, sir," she suggested.

"I'll write it down."

The water and the presence of other people seemed to give Harriet a little strength. The colour was slowly returning to her face and she was able to sit up against an armchair.

"Lessing was married to my sister. He killed her. He left her alone and in pain to die in the cold. She had a broken leg and no way of getting help." Harriet started to weep and then cried out in pain, clutching her belly. "I need my medication — the morphine. It's on there by my notes."

Calladine took the phial of liquid and poured it into the empty glass. Harriet drank it down.

"The ambulance is coming up the street, sir," said Ruth, at the door. "I'll go and meet them."

"Harriet," Calladine said, supporting her shoulders. "We think Lessing was involved in the kidnapping of two little girls."

She grabbed his arm. Despite her weakened state she still had quite a grip. "He took them, I'm sure of it. He worked with a rogue called Yuri. If they're still alive and still in the country then he'll have put them somewhere."

"Yuri who? Do you know anything about him?"

"No — but Gordon's been helping him for years. Gordon has a couple of lorries — *Lessing Transport*. He can travel all over the place and no one asks any questions."

"Where's his place? Where does he work from?"

"The industrial estate, off the bypass. He keeps the lorries there."

Harriet cried out in pain again and her head slumped forward. Two paramedics walked into the room.

One of them picked up her notes and quickly scanned through them. "We'll take her to the General," he told his colleague.

"We should send someone with her," Ruth told Calladine. "I'll arrange for a uniform to meet them in the ED and keep an eye on her."

Calladine doubted that Harriet Finch would try to do a runner, or be up to killing anyone else, but he knew he should follow protocol. She might seem harmless now, but she was still a killer. He and Ruth had a quick look round the house. Everything was neat and tidy. There was no sign of anything untoward.

"You the police?" One of the paramedics came back inside.

Calladine nodded.

"She's pretty high on morphine but she's insisting there's a dead 'un in the shed." He grinned. "We hear all sorts so don't take it too literally."

"The shed, you say?" Calladine gave Ruth a humourless smile. Harriet was probably telling the truth. "We'd better take a look."

The two of them walked out through the back door and across the neat garden. Calladine rattled the shed door but it was locked. The structure was soundly built but made entirely of wood. "Pass me that spade." He nodded at the object lying against the fence. He raised it high and slammed it into the narrow gap between the door and the side of the shed. The door splintered and sprang open — he'd smashed the lock.

They saw the tarpaulin immediately. There was obviously something underneath it. Calladine took hold of a corner and pulled tentatively.

"Jayden North."

He was lying in a pool of his own blood and there was a nasty wound to his neck. Harriet Finch had killed five people. Yet she was frail, weak and in constant need of medication. What was it that had kept her going?

Ruth put a hand to the uninjured side of his neck and nodded. "No pulse and he's cold, sir."

"How did she manage it? So much death caused by someone so fragile." He shuddered. "I don't understand how Harriet Finch could get the upper hand physically against someone like him."

"She'd nothing to lose — that must be it."

"But why him? With the others she was on a mission, righting wrongs. So why did Jayden North become a victim?"

"He surprised her?" Ruth suggested. "Imogen may have said something when she spoke to him. If he knew stuff, if he thought Harriet was responsible for his uncle's death then he might have come looking."

"She wouldn't have seemed much of a threat either." Calladine pulled a face. "How wrong he was, and he paid for his mistake with his life."

"We need to get the doc down here, sir. Uniform have arrived. I'll get them to seal the place."

\* \* \*

According to information found by Rocco, Gordon Lessing rented a small office and two large parking spaces on the industrial estate.

"We need to get down there," Calladine decided.

"You mean before Greco digs out the same information?"

"Look — we're almost there. The murders are sorted now and given these new facts we shouldn't waste time trying to contact a DI who could be anywhere. It's only down the road from us, after all."

"In that case I won't argue. But if this goes all pear shaped, you're picking up the flack, right?"

Calladine smiled and grabbed his coat.

Lessing's office was empty and the unopened mail had gathered behind the door. The windows were so dirty, it looked like nobody had used the place in months.

"Uses it as a front, d'you think?"

"Don't know, Ruth but it doesn't look good. If he was keeping the girls here then you'd expect him to visit, carry on as normal. They'd need food and water at the very least."

"Oh this is normal," a female voice replied from behind them. "We never see him from one week's end to the next."

"Do you work for Mr Lessing?" Calladine asked.

"No — for the engineering firm next door, I'm what passes for admin. The reality is that the owner's my son." She smiled.

Calladine got out his warrant card and showed it to the woman. "According to our records Lessing has this office and two parking spaces for his lorries. Are they out at the moment?"

"God no — I don't think they've moved in weeks. How he can call this shambles a business, I don't know. But then again he must be doing something right. You should see the car he drives. It makes no sense. He must make money doing something, but it's got nowt to do with haulage."

"So where are they, the lorries?" Ruth asked. "Shouldn't they be parked here?"

"They used to be, but they got in everyone's way — old decrepit things they are. He's parked them up round the back somewhere — on a piece of spare land. Like I said, they haven't moved in ages."

"We should take a look." Calladine gestured to Ruth. "Give me a minute — I want to get some things from the car."

He opened the boot and took out a long screwdriver and a bunch of keys. Then they walked off along a path that took them around to the rear of the buildings. Once round the back the path disappeared and they were soon stepping over some very rough ground. Calladine knew the land stretched out for some way, all the way back to the bypass in fact.

"It's a bit wild in here. Watch your step!" he called to Ruth. "Don't want you falling, not in your condition."

"You can stop all that before you even get started."

"Sorry, but I don't want to be responsible for any mishaps. The long grass is covering a lot of rubble. There's all sorts of rubbish lying around. Watch you don't stand on a broken bottle. Some idiots have been using the land as a tip."

"That's the Hobfield." Ruth nodded towards the tower blocks that stood a few hundred yards away. "But there are notices."

Calladine shook his head. "Lucky if the little bastards can read. Even if they could, they'd pay no heed."

"There, sir." Ruth pointed.

The two lorries were parked up in front of them. The woman had been right — neither of them was going anywhere. One had two tyres missing and grass was growing as high as one of the back doors of the other. It looked like no one had been near them in ages.

"What are we looking for, sir?" Ruth asked.

Calladine felt a shiver travel along his spine. "I don't like this. It's too quiet back here and it's well sheltered by those trees." He nodded.

"Yeah. You could come and go, do what you like and no one would see."

Calladine rapped with the screwdriver on the side of one of the lorries while Ruth walked around the other.

"There are greasy fingerprints on the doors here," she called to him, "and relatively fresh footprints too, in the mud. See, the ground has frozen over leaving a perfect imprint."

"So someone has been here." He knocked again.

"We should get Julian down here — he needs to look at this," Ruth said.

"We don't know what we've got yet," he replied, taking hold of a backdoor handle and pulling. "Locked."

"If it wasn't, half the kids from the estate would be hanging out in there."

"We need to get both these lorries open and take a look inside."

"Lessing has been murdered. We know he's involved in the kidnapping, so call for backup. You can't do this on your own."

171

"I'm not alone — you're here with me."

"This is really about Greco, isn't it? But sooner or later you are going to have to let him in."

"If you call Julian, then Stephen Greco will be down here in a flash."

"Possibly not. Remember, Greco is outsourcing forensics to the Duggan Centre. You can imagine how Julian will feel about that!"

Calladine was only half listening to her. He was looking through the bunch of keys he'd brought with him.

"This one."

He tried the key in the lock on the door handle but it only turned so far. He pulled again but had no luck. Calladine rammed the screwdriver into the gap between both doors trying to lever them apart. The doors were rusty so he might be in with a chance.

After five or so minutes of pushing and banging he was in. The back doors sprang open, filling the cavernous interior with light. The smell hit them first. For a few seconds it made them both feel queasy, mostly at the prospect of finding two small bodies inside. Calladine's heart was pounding. God knows how Ruth felt. This was the part of the job he hated most of all. There was nothing worse than crimes involving children.

"It's a chemical smell," Ruth said at last, surprised.

"Reminds me of caravan holidays when I was a kid," Calladine said, squinting as he tried to see.

"A chemical toilet, that's what it is," Ruth realised. "Look, guv, right at the end, on the floor."

Calladine climbed in. The lorry wasn't big enough for him to stand so he crawled across to what looked like a heap of rags on the floor.

"I think it's them!" he called back.

Reluctantly, because of what he might find he carefully removed an almost threadbare blanket and saw the two girls. They were still in their school uniforms and huddled together for warmth. Neither of them was conscious, but both were breathing.

"Time to get that help you wanted, and quick!" he called back to Ruth. "They're here, both of them. They're cold but breathing. I think they've been drugged."

Ruth was on her phone immediately, calling for the ambulance. Then she rang Julian.

Calladine took off his coat and placed it over the girls. He looked towards Ruth. She was still on the phone. He didn't need her to say anything; he knew what she was doing. She'd be speaking to Greco.

Within fifteen minutes the rough tract of land was filled with people, all active. The paramedics took the girls away in an ambulance. Julian and his forensics people were crawling all over the place, when Greco arrived.

Calladine groaned inwardly. The young DI had a face like thunder.

"This is my case, Calladine." He spat the words out. "At the very least you should have told me what you were up to."

"I had no idea I'd find them here. But I'm not going to apologise for doing so. You should have been more forthcoming with your information. The body on the footpath was a man called Yuri Arcos and apparently Vice at Central knows him. That means your dark net people knew him too but you said nothing."

"How did you find this place?"

"Harriet Finch told me about it."

"Who the hell is she?"

"She's Lessing's sister-in-law. She's our bucket-list killer, or tarot-card killer — take your pick."

"So the cases are linked?"

"Yes. I did say as much, but you didn't want me involved — remember?"

He felt Ruth give him a discreet kick on the back of the shin. "Sir, we should go and speak to Harriet. Don't forget how ill she is."

"Okay. Our job here's done anyway."

He gave Greco a self-satisfied smile and walked off after Ruth.

"Big headed prick. What is it with him?"

"Simple, guv — nothing, but you still don't like him, do you? You're behaving like a child and it doesn't suit you."

"Solved the case though, didn't we? And with no input from Greco."

"That was down to Harriet," she reminded him.

"What time is it?"

"Why, have you got somewhere else to be?" Ruth asked sarcastically.

"Actually I have, and I don't want to be late."

"We'll go to the hospital, check on the girls, look in on Harriet Finch then you can go and do whatever. How does that suit you?"

"I'll drive," he said. "And stop getting at me. I've got a lot on my mind."

"A lot on your mind! That's rich, given that most of it's your own doing. Lydia, Eve Walker, and Greco — you bring it on yourself."

"You know it's not really my fault . . ." he tried.

"Oh yes it is. You've been in a funny mood for a day or two and it's affecting how you are at work. The women in your life, your new-found family, you can blame any one of them. But you need to sort it out."

"Perhaps it's down to the job. Perhaps I came back too soon. I must have got more of a shock than I realised when Fallon shot me and I banged my head."

"Stop whining and make your peace with Greco. You're going to have to eventually — you know that, don't you, sir?"

\* \* \*

They pulled into the hospital car park.

"I suppose I'll get used to him," he sighed. "He's obviously thorough, but he's a tad slow for my liking. I mean he should be here too, but I don't see his car."

"He'll be bothering Julian, trying to get rid of him or making sure he doesn't miss anything. What's happening with him, your one-time cousin? You haven't mentioned him in a while."

"He's banged up," he replied with a smile on his face. "You know, Ruth, that's so good to say. And this time he hasn't got a cat in hell's chance of getting out."

\* \* \*

Calladine flashed his warrant card at the receptionist, not that he needed to; she knew very well who he was.

"Where are the girls?" he asked.

"Paediatrics, second floor." As they walked up the stairs, Ruth had begun to flag. "Bloody pregnancy," she moaned. "Seems to sap all my energy. Most days I'm dead on my feet by teatime."

"Me too and I'm not pregnant." He laughed. "Just getting old, perhaps too bloody old."

"Is that what's bothering you?" Ruth asked him. "Do you see Stephen Greco as a threat, a future you don't feel part of?"

"Don't be daft, he's got no experience."

"He has enough, and he's into all the new stuff the force is introducing."

"Nothing wrong with the old stuff — always worked for me."

The two girls were in adjoining rooms. A female PC had been assigned to monitor conversations between them. It was a way of finding out small details they might be reluctant to talk about.

In the corridor outside their rooms, the doctor greeted Calladine with a nod. "The parents are with them."

"How are they? Are they hurt in any way?"

Calladine dreaded hearing what the doctor might say in reply. "They've been given something, a tranquillizer, I suspect, but nothing more. From what Isla Prideau told her mother, they appear to have slept for most of the time. Someone brought them a little food and water but only twice, she thinks."

"Have either of them been injured or abused?"

"No, Inspector, they are both okay. They have been examined and we found nothing untoward, and there is no sign of sexual interference. They're still sleepy but I'm sure that that will have worn off by tomorrow."

He heard Ruth exhale in relief.

"Their clothes will need to go to forensics," Calladine told him.

"An officer has already bagged them up, Inspector."

"They're safe, Tom. We found them, and got them out," Ruth said. "And it was down to you."

"Too close for comfort, though. Any longer and it could have been a different story. They'd have been left there to die." He shuddered.

Leah Cassidy's mother was weeping. Calladine couldn't imagine why. Her daughter was safe, unhurt — she'd been lucky.

"It was my fault," she told them. "I put that stupid photo on the website. It was only so my friends could see what a big girl she was — going off to school in her uniform."

"He was a seasoned predator, Mrs Cassidy. You weren't to know," Ruth consoled her.

"This has been the worst time of my entire life. I thought I'd lost her," she sobbed.

"She needs to rest." The doctor patted the woman on her shoulder.

"I can't leave her. I'll never be able to leave her again."

"Harriet Finch?" Ruth asked the doctor.

"Okay — we'll go find her."

There was no point staying with the children until they were fully awake and by that time Greco would have his people in place.

Harriet had been given a large dose of morphine and was barely conscious. Her friend Nesta sat by her bedside along with a young woman Calladine didn't know.

"Jane Lessing. I'm Harriet's niece."

"Lessing?" Ruth asked.

"Gordon Lessing was my father," she told them. "Aunt Harriet is all that's left of my family now, and from the looks of things, she won't be with us for much longer."

"You do know what Harriet did?" asked Ruth.

"She killed him. She lured him down into that cellar of his and left him to die."

"But you're still here, supporting her?"

"Not from choice, but Nesta insisted. Harriet told some story about him killing my mother," she shook her head. "I can't see it, but on the other hand, Harriet is a good woman. She wouldn't say that unless she knew, really knew." Jane Lessing wiped the tears from her eyes. "I know my father had secrets, that he hid things from me and Mum. So what am I supposed to think? I'm here because she's dying. I will get the truth once you lot have everything sorted. So I will stay open-minded."

"We will make sure that you're kept up to date with everything," Ruth reassured her.

"The cancer has spread to her brain so what with that and the medication she's nothing like her old self. You aren't going to whip her away and lock her up, are you?"

"No, she'll stay here until . . . until the end," Calladine said sadly. "She will have a police guard, a PC on the door, but it's just protocol."

Harriet Finch would not escape. They'd be lucky if she lasted the night.

# CHAPTER 20

"You get off home. It's been quite a day and you look exhausted."

"Thanks, Tom. I think I'll do just that," Ruth agreed. "And you get some proper sleep tonight. No gallivanting off with that new woman of yours now."

She was right. He needed some time out but he doubted he'd get it. He checked his watch. Nearly seven; he should pick up Amy. Luckily Ruth had gone, so he didn't have to explain himself.

Calladine had planned to go home and change — make an effort, but the exhibition finished at eight so he didn't have time. After a quick goodnight to the team he left them to it. He decided to take his car and leave it outside Amy's for the night. She had invited him to stay, after all. Things were looking up. He should feel better, but he didn't.

She greeted him with, "You still look dreadful, grey around the gills. If you're not careful, Tom, the job will make you ill."

More advice he didn't need. "I'll be fine. I need a little feet up time, that's all. But despite the way I look it's been a productive day. We caught our killer, and found the two little girls." He smiled.

"That's great news!" She kissed his cheek. "The girls — they're okay?"

"They'd been drugged and they were very cold when we found them, but yes, they're fine, or they will be."

"You're a good man." She kissed him again. "You do a dangerous job. Did your killer get rough?"

"Hardly." He smiled. "Our killer is a very sick older woman. In fact I'm surprised she had the strength to do what she did."

"Prison is still too good for her," Amy retorted.

"She'll never see the inside of a prison. I doubt she'll last much longer — she has terminal cancer."

"A deadly imperfection, that's cancer," she said thoughtfully. "But why kill those people? I don't understand — and why the cards?"

"We know why she killed — she wanted her own brand of justice. It was payback time for incidents from the past, crimes left unpunished. But the cards . . ." He shrugged. "My theory is that they were left to ensure that we pinned the killings on a single person. The methods were all different, you see. There was no common element, as there is with most serial killers."

Amy shuddered. "We should go. You need to think about something else — relax a bit. I'm sure all this involvement with cold-hearted killers does you no good at all."

He took her hand as they left the shop and walked the few hundred yards to the community centre.

"You might see something you like, perhaps something by a local artist." Amy put to him.

"We'll see what's on offer. But you want to go, so that's good enough for me." Art wasn't really his thing, but it was Amy's. Anyway there was free drink — as good a reason as any to give it a whirl.

The exhibition had been open since three that afternoon and a number of the paintings adorning the walls in the main hall had little red stickers on them. The local art group and independent artists had had a good day. Calladine browsed as Amy went to get them a glass of wine each. There were many pictures of local scenes. Some were of the surrounding countryside and hills, which were pretty but clichéd. It was the gritty depictions of the towns, particularly Leesdon and the Hobfield that got his attention. He was particularly drawn to one of them. It had a raw realism he could identify with.

"Good, isn't it?" a woman's voice asked from behind him.

Calladine simply nodded but didn't look round. Something about the picture had captured his imagination. The artist had caught the atmosphere of that hellhole, the Hobfield.

"Art doesn't interest me, as a rule, but this is good. He's really caught the feel of the place."

"The young man has real talent. He's an employee of my son's — well, was an employee." She laughed lightly. "Now we're sponsoring him through university so he can do a fine art degree. So he's lost to the pharmaceutical business, I fear."

Up until that moment Calladine hadn't really taken much notice, but now the hairs on the back of his neck prickled. He turned around slowly, his heart pounding. It was Eve Walker.

"I know who you are, Tom. I've always known. I've always lived locally so how could I not? I hoped that one day we'd meet and have the opportunity to talk, but while your mother was still alive I didn't have the right. I'd made promises, you see."

"So what gives you the right now?" he asked, his face hardening into a grim frown.

"Because Freda is gone and you know the truth. That was also part of the deal. You must be curious — I know I am."

"Tom, you okay?" Amy asked, appearing with two glasses of red wine.

"Yep — fine. I like this one," he said, turning to the picture, and completely ignoring Eve. "Reminds of my job. It'd look good on the wall in my office."

"It's already sold, Tom," Amy pointed out. "Red sticker — see."

"Actually I bought that one," Eve told her. "I would be only too happy to give it to you, Inspector. Be my guest, take it, hang it on your wall."

Calladine didn't say a word. He took the wine and strode off in the direction of the small anteroom where people had put their coats.

"I'm sorry," Amy apologised. "He's not normally so rude. I think he's had a heavy day. Perhaps I shouldn't have brought him here."

"The fault is entirely mine," Eve Walker insisted. "I should never have spoken to him in the first place. It's too soon . . ."

"Why — what did you say? Does he know you?"

"Yes, well, no, but he knows who I am. It's a difficult situation."

The woman was somewhere in her seventies, not that her age detracted from her attractiveness. She was tall. Her hair was straight, medium-length and still dark. She had neat features and high cheekbones, and she was expensively dressed.

"Are you a relative?" Amy asked. "I ask, because I see a resemblance. I think he looks like you."

Eve smiled and lowered her eyes.

"Yes, I am," she admitted. "But he obviously doesn't want to know me, not yet anyway."

"You said the two of you had never spoken. If you're related and local, how can that be?"

Eve Walker said nothing, looking away towards the other room.

"You and Tom, you are connected, despite what you say . . ." Amy half closed her eyes for a moment. "You are the reason he's been so preoccupied recently. The other day he was in my shop and I gave him an impromptu reading. You're the Queen of Pentacles! I should have known." She put down her wine on the nearest table and went to find Tom.

"You can't hide away in here all evening," Amy said, shutting the door behind her and leaning against it. "She's the one you're scared of, isn't she?"

"I'm not scared — I just can't do this yet."

"Who is she, Tom? She's a relative, I guessed that much; you look like her."

Tom Calladine looked Amy full in the face. Was it that obvious? All these years — who else had noticed? he wondered.

"Has she gone?" he asked.

"I don't think so, but what of it? You're behaving like a child. Whatever demons these are you need to face them head on. Do that and you'll feel so much better."

It was good advice, but could he act on it? Could he let Eve Walker, Buckley as she was now, into his life?

"She's my birth mother." He spoke slowly. "But until today we'd never met, never spoken. I've only known about her for a few months, since Freda — my mother — died. She left me that tin, the one you kept for me. It contains all the gory details about my parentage."

Amy's blue eyes widened. "That's some secret, Tom. You should go and speak to her; she seems nice. She'll be as uncomfortable about the situation as you are. You need to stop hiding from this and get out there."

She sounded just like Ruth — making him feel like a naughty kid!

"Will you come with me?"

She smiled and reached for his hand. "Of course I will. Do this and you won't regret it. You were meant to meet her. It was in the cards — remember? The Queen of Pentacles."

"Not sure about all that . . . but I don't know what I'll say. Part of me hates her, but the other part, the sensible side of me knows it's not her fault. She was just doing what my parents wanted — keeping out of my life."

"Your parents are gone now. Meeting her can't hurt anyone. She's over there," Amy said, opening the door and peering out. "Come on, let's go and say hello properly."

This was one of the most difficult things he'd ever had to do. If Amy had not been at his side he'd probably have done a runner.

Eve Walker, or Buckley, was gazing at the painting he'd admired so much.

"It's very good of you to let me have it. You must let me pay," he said politely.

She spun round and gave him a dazzling smile, "I wouldn't hear of it. Take it with you when you leave." She stared into his face for several seconds. "Do you want to talk, Tom? There's a lot I'd like to say to you."

"Not really." He cleared his throat. "I know we'll have to at some stage. Don't misunderstand me," he added hurriedly. "I do have questions; it's the answers I might not like. That's what's stopping me."

She put a comforting hand on his arm. "All in good time, then. There's no rush. We have a lot of catching up to do."

Tom Calladine looked into the face of the woman who'd given birth to him, and smiled tentatively. Eve Walker was a looker now, so he could only imagine how beautiful she must have been when his dad knew her. He'd never really thought about it but perhaps his dad had had the same trouble with women that he did. Eve was his Lydia and Freda . . . ?

Freda Calladine had been his father's rock, his steadying influence. She'd guided him, taken him in hand. She'd run their home, worked, and loved him and his dad unconditionally. He looked at Eve Walker. No matter what she turned out to be like — no matter how fond of her he might become over time — Freda Calladine would always be his mother. Ruth had been right about that — he should have listened to her.

His sergeant had always been his voice of reason.

**THE END**

# CHARACTER LIST

**Detective Inspector Tom Calladine**
He is single, just past fifty. He is tall, slim build but with reasonable muscle tone, his hair used to be dark but is now greying and is cut close to his head. His daughter is called Zoe, she resulted from his short-lived marriage and he only found about her recently.

**Detective Sergeant Ruth Bayliss**
She is single in *Dead Wrong* but meets someone — teacher Jake Ireson, in *Dead Silent*. She's in her mid-thirties, likes bird-watching. Works with Calladine at Leesdon police station.

**Detective Constable Simon Rockliffe — Rocco**
A solid team member. He works hard and gets results. He is tipped to go far. He was attacked on the Hobfield in *Dead Wrong*.

**Detective Constable Imogen Goode**
She is the IT expert of the team. She is intense — very keen on her work — a bit of a nerd. She is being eyed up by Julian — the forensics expert.

**Acting Detective Chief Inspector Brad Long**
Overweight, and generally lazy — formerly the other team leader in the police station.

**Detective Inspector Stephen Greco**
Detective at nearby Oldston police station. Ambitious.

**Doctor Sebastian Hoyle**
Pathologist. Often referred to as the doc.

**Forensic scientist — Doctor Julian Batho**
Unmarried, hard-working. Not particularly good-looking.

**Monika Smith**
Care home manager and former girlfriend of Calladine.

**Freda Calladine**
Tom's late mother — was resident in the care home run by Monika.

**Lydia Holden**
Reporter seeking the big time. She is a glamorous blonde who uses her looks to get what she wants. Calladine falls for her. She was a reporter for the *Leesworth Echo* in the case described in *Dead Wrong*.

**Ray Fallon**
Calladine's cousin on his mother's side. One of Manchester's most notorious gangsters — drugs, gun running — whatever he can make money at. His gang provides the drugs for the local housing estate — the Hobfield. Shot Calladine in *Dead Silent*. In prison awaiting trial.

**Amy "Amaris" Dean**
Seductive owner of Starshine shop selling tarot cards and other esoterica.

# THE JOFFE BOOKS STORY

We began in 2014 when Jasper agreed to publish his mum's much-rejected romance novel and it became a bestseller.

Since then we've grown into the largest independent publisher in the UK. We're extremely proud to publish some of the very best writers in the world, including Joy Ellis, Faith Martin, Caro Ramsay, Helen Forrester, Simon Brett and Robert Goddard. Everyone at Joffe Books loves reading and we never forget that it all begins with the magic of an author telling a story.

We are proud to publish talented first-time authors, as well as established writers whose books we love introducing to a new generation of readers.

We won Trade Publisher of the Year at the Independent Publishing Awards in 2023 and Best Publisher Award in 2024 at the People's Book Prize. We have been shortlisted for Independent Publisher of the Year at the British Book Awards for the last five years, and were shortlisted for the Diversity and Inclusivity Award at the 2022 Independent Publishing Awards. In 2023 we were shortlisted for Publisher of the Year at the RNA Industry Awards, and in 2024 we were shortlisted at the CWA Daggers for the Best Crime and Mystery Publisher.

We built this company with your help, and we love to hear from you, so please email us about absolutely anything bookish at feedback@joffebooks.com.

If you want to receive free books every Friday and hear about all our new releases, join our mailing list here: www.joffebooks.com/freebooks.

And when you tell your friends about us, just remember: it's pronounced Joffe as in coffee or toffee!